City of Kings

by

Rosario Castellanos

Translated by Robert S. Rudder
and
Gloria Chacón de Arjona

Introduction by Claudia Schaefer

City of Kings

by

Rosario Castellanos

Translated by Robert S. Rudder
and
Gloria Chacón de Arjona

Introduction by Claudia Schaefer

LATIN AMERICAN LITERARY REVIEW PRESS
SERIES: DISCOVERIES
PITTSBURGH, PENNSYLVANIA

1992

The Latin American Literary Review Press publishes Latin American creative writing under the series title *Discoveries*, and critical works under the series title *Explorations*.

Library of Congress Cataloging-in-Publication Data

Castellanos, Rosario.
[Ciudad Real. English]
City of Kings / by Rosario Castellanos ; translated by Gloria Chacón de Arjona and Robert S. Rudder ; introduction by Claudia Schaefer.
p. cm. -- (Series Discoveries)
ISBN 0-935480-63-3
1. San Cristóbal de las Casas (Mexico)--Fiction. I. Chacón de Arjona, Gloria. II. Rudder, Robert S. III. Schaefer, Claudia, 1949- . IV. Title. V. Series: Discoveries.
PQ7297.C2596C513 1993
863--dc20 92-21223
CIP

Ciudad Real was originally published in Spanish by Universidad Veracruzana, 1960. Reprinted as a coedition, Universidad Veracruzana - Edicones La Letra, 1990. ELL: Antonio de Sola No. 46, Col. Condesa, C.P. 06140, Mexico, D.F., A.P. 40-290 TEL 256-20-10

The paper used in this publication meets the minimum requirements of the American National Standard for Permanence of Paper for Printed Library Materials Z39.48-1984.(∞)

Cover illustration from mural by Rolando Arjona Amábilis, Hotel Carrousel, Cancún, Mexico.

City of Kings may be ordered directly from the publisher:
Latin American Literary Review Press
2300 Palmer Street, Pittsburgh, PA 15218
Tel (412) 351-1477 • Fax (412) 351-6831

ACKNOWLEDGEMENTS

This project is supported in part by grants from the National Endowment for the Arts in Washington, D.C., a federal agency, and the Commonwealth of Pennsylvania Council on the Arts.

Special thanks to Professor Kathleen Ross for her excellent editing of the manuscript.

Dedicated to
the *Instituto Nacional Indigenista,*
that works to change the conditions
in which my people live.

On what day? During what moon? In what year did these things which are told here come to pass? As in dreams, as in nightmares, everything is simultaneous, everything is present, everything exists today.

CONTENTS

Introduction

A writer capable of plotting the most superbly ironic of situations for her characters and a woman deeply aware of her own role in the everyday ironies of the Mexican social reality in which she lived and wrote, Rosario Castellanos would undoubtedly find a certain amount of joyful paradox in the translation of *Ciudad real* [*City of Kings*] (1960) for an English-speaking audience during the time of the five hundredth anniversary of Columbus' fateful landing on the American continent. For were it not for the act of the translator, the cultural intermediary, we perhaps could not even begin to fathom how historical events would have transpired or been reported through the centuries; and were it not for Castellanos' painfully self-conscious awareness of her own acts of cultural interpretation, we as readers would lose the rich texture of ambiguity which so permeates the relationships between the cultures of which she speaks.

The beauty—as well as the tragic irony—of Castellanos' stories in this collection and indeed of her entire written legacy to us is that while it was her fate to witness the first moments of the birth of modern Mexico as a nation in the 1930s and 1940s under the leadership of Lázaro Cárdenas and others, she simultaneously became aware of the personal sacrifices necessary to form and maintain that vision of a social collectivity. In *City of Kings*, as in numerous other narratives, Castellanos posits many of the crucial issues regarding identity, ethnicity, class, and community which have made a reappearance now, in the last decade of the twentieth century, within, along, and even beyond the borders of Mexico itself.

Her own status as a *ladina* or white woman of mixed (European and indigenous) ancestry who belonged to a family of wealthy landowners in Chiapas, then as a university-educated woman in mid century Mexico whose sentimental ties to her region had not been severed even though her economic ones had disappeared along with her father's expropriated possessions, and finally as an intellectual whose participation in official government programs both in the interest of the indigenous communities in Mexico and to benefit Mexico's interests abroad (as cultural ambassador to Israel and indirect sponsor for her country's petroleum industry there) placed her in a position of privilege which she never ceased to question. We find her often futile search for answers played out across the pages of her novels, short stories, essays, newspaper articles, theatrical works, and abundant collections of poetry. While trying to live up to her own ideals of gender, societal, and economic equality, Castellanos apprises us of the constant barrage of impediments she faces in putting these ideas into practice, especially in terms of the inevitable and frequently violent encounters between different cultural groups within the same national boundaries. As a result, her writings take on an autobiographical dimension, with each instance depicted showing the results of the individual or collective exercise of power over the powerless victim and each text having as its narrative axis—either directly or indirectly—the experiences of Castellanos herself.

The overwhelming sense of guilt which erupts from this ambiguous position as participant and critic at the same time is evident in her use of narrators trapped by their own naïveté and storytellers ultimately finding themselves outsiders, excluded from "belonging" except in their identification with the pain and suffering of *all* victims—in particular, women, children, and the Amerindians. In one of her frequent confessional moments, Castellanos remarks that the literary consequence of this social alienation is embodied in the tone of sarcastic humor which invades most if not all of what she writes, what she calls "the claw mark of ferocious humor" inspired by the duality of the urgent need to write (in order to feel alive) and the frustration with the problematic contents of that very writing. In her own version of the popular saying about not being able to teach an old dog new tricks, however, Castellanos declares that she must go on doing what she does best, like "a dinosaur that can't change its skin or species" she insists on using the power of the written word to exorcise her own ghosts with the hope that someone some day will read the results. By embodying this sacrificial yet culturally productive role in several of her characters, Rosario Castellanos vividly portrays what Mexican novelist Carlos Fuentes has referred to as "las buenas conciencias," those who live haunted by the vision of social injustice around them while recognizing that their "good intentions" effect little real change in the status quo; they prick the collective conscience of society with their words but are often themselves consumed in the process. Cut short by a tragic accident in 1974, Castellanos' life and works are imbued with such overtones of well-intentioned thoughts and proposals in defense of human rights and women's rights which she witnessed dashed on the rocks of a patriarchal family, a patriarchal state, and an institutionalized religious hierarchy with no "good intentions" of their own to relinquish any of their power.

As part of the group of writers in the Mexican capital commonly referred to as the "Generation of 1950" and which included such important literary figures as Emilio Carballido, Jaime Sabines, Ernesto Cardenal, and Augusto Monterroso, Rosario Castellanos shared many of their social and cultural preoccupations; but she stood out as a lone voice working through on a personal level many of the problems *and* potentialities of what in the 1990s we might want to call a feminist politics. Marriage, motherhood, the relationships between parents and children, and the attraction of a professional career all enter into her scrutiny, yet she never separates these issues from the broader Mexican social perspective. Indeed, several of the stories in the present volume have female protagonists—among them "The Truce," "Modesta Gómez," "The Fourth Vigil," and "The Wheel of Hunger"—but the fact that they are all women proves to be a *double* burden since they are all Indians as well and therefore must submit to two orders of control over their bodies: male authority and the power of the *ladino* or *mestizo*. Thus hunger, economic servitude, persecution, abuse, the ramifications of offering or accepting charity, and the fight for cultural survival are what lie beneath the relationships sketched out in the ten stories of *City of Kings*.

Along with the two novels *Balún Canán* [*The Nine Guardians*] (1957) and *Oficio de tinieblas* [*Office of Tenebrae*] (1962) and the volume of short stories entitled *Los convidados de agosto* [*The Guests of August*] (1964), *City of Kings* completes what has been called the "Chiapas Cycle" in Castellanos' fictional works. As part of the important literary project of *indigenista* narratives in Latin America, one which includes works by Miguel Angel Asturias, Ermilo Abreu Gómez, and Eraclio Zepeda as well and whose most remote roots some trace back to sixteenth century Fray Bartolomé de Las Casas' defense of the native inhabitants of the Americas as human beings rather than the savage beasts condemned by the European conquerors, *City of*

Kings reflects this writer's valuable contribution to the general (and radical) attempt to articulate the literary text with the indigenous world of the "zona maya." This ancient cultural and geographic zone's communal identity is centered around a common linguistic family of Mayan languages and a ceremonial religious tradition based on agricultural cultivation; it does not correspond directly to any one modern national entity but instead extends along the Mexican states of Chiapas, Tabasco, Campeche, and Yucatan, through Quintana Roo, across the republics of Guatemala and Belize, all the way into the territory of Honduras. Born into a family of provincial wealth tied to landholdings in Comitán, Chiapas, a small town on the Mexican border with Guatemala many of whose current residents still preserve dialects derived from the Mayan linguistic tree, Castellanos chooses key cities for the native populations of this state as focal points for the narrative settings of her *indigenista* novels and stories.

She returns time and time again to that region of well-documented historical resistance to the colonizing forces from Spain and, more recently, the site of failed federal projects to integrate the indigenous populations (forming a majority of the area's inhabitants almost always) into the cultural and economic universe of the *ladino* ruling classes. Without the *real* possibility of immersing herself completely in the world of these Tzotzil-Tzeltal groups—in spite of her contact with them through her work in the National Indigenous Institute and her direction of its pedagogical outreach programs to "Castilianize" the natives during the 1950s—Castellanos turns to the foundational myths of the *Popol Vuh* and other sacred Mayan texts to create the most vivid (and perhaps most clearly recognizable to other Mexicans) possible suggestion of these cultures for the Spanish speaking reader. (She, of course, reads the Spanish version of the Mayan mythology.) These origin myths of the Maya-Quiché become one of the fundamental sources from which a basic timeless cosmovision and a popular speech put in the mouths of indigenous characters are extracted. The second stimulus for the narratives is an honorable and fervent desire to address the need to resolve the political, social and economic problem of the "Maya Zone" which has left the descendants of the original native populations at a dead end for decades, if not more accurately centuries, with regard to a decent level of existence; this "problem" has also left the centralized federal government in Mexico City with an unresolved and frequently volatile situation in the more distant provinces. The two elements—the somewhat exotic mythic universe of the historical Maya and the actual life-and-death struggles of their contemporary descendants—function side by side in the composition of Castellanos' works.

In the dedication of the Spanish language version of *City of Kings* we find the author's overt statement of faith in the government bureau established under President Cárdenas to reform the laws of property, land, and citizenship for all the inhabitants of that region of the country: "[I dedicate this] to the National Indigenous Institute, which is working to change the living conditions of *my people*" (emphasis added). Castellanos' willing assumption of the role of cultural interpreter and defender of the natives of Chiapas, along with her adoption of them as "her people" with whom some type of bond has been created either by accident (birth) or choice (her return as cultural liaison), are echoed in several of the well-meaning characters of the stories in *City of Kings*: the doctor and his female assistant at the Indian Aid Mission (in "The Wheel of Hunger"), the anthropologist at the Mission of Charity ("The Gift, Refused"), and the linguistic expert brought in to translate the Bible into Tzeltal for the "Organization" in the highlands of Chiapas ("Arthur Smith Finds Salvation"). Whether or not Castellanos arrived at conclusions similar to those reached by these individuals—representing the medical establishment, the intellectual community, and organized religion, three of the institutions traditionally charged with the mission of "changing for the better" the lives of indigenous peoples—is hard to say. In purely literary terms, however, each of these three instances is premised on some "need" of a community of "others" for which one's own culture seems to offer the best (and only?) solution, a relationship of power suspiciously like that of the National Indigenous Institute and its street theater workshops to promote "education by assimilation" into *mestizo* culture. And each of the three closes with a solidifying of the distance between the cultures of the protagonists, just as the streets of The City of Kings are divided into separate zones for the Indians and for the *mestizos*, and the fertile valleys are claimed for the *ladinos* while the natives live perched on the arid mountaintops. In the end, the doctor, the anthropologist, and the linguist all fail miserably in their attempts at communication with and acculturation of the Indians, both individually and collectively, and all retreat into the very structures of power that have historically contributed to holding these cultures in contentious encounter. It is left up to the conscience of the reader to deal with the personal motivations of these characters as well as with the dilemma of their obviously sentimental attachment to the charitable relationship between well-meaning *ladinos* (and all of them do *not* mean well in Castellanos' stories) and the objectified Indian. What survives as an overall characteristic of these tales is their dramatic irony—the space between thought and act, between theory and practice, between innocence and disillusionment. The translators of this volume have done an admirable job with the difficult task of capturing the ironic innuendos and the differences in tone and language of the two communities portrayed. José Antonio Romero, student of anthropology from an urban university, volunteer in The City of Kings to mediate disputes between feuding towns, detailed observer of local customs, and generous to a fault, ends up asking himself (although he actually appears to be addressing the reader directly since he says "What I want *you* to tell me is this . . .") a series of questions that serve to sum up this cultural rift: "Did I, as a professional, as a man, do something wrong? There must have been something. Something I didn't know how to *give* them." We can begin to examine the reception (or rejection) of his acts of benevolence by focusing our attention on this single verb.

Clustered around the unifying image of The City of Kings, ancient name of the city of San Cristóbal de Las Casas and cultural center for the Chamulas, the ten narratives of this collection are inserted into clearly historical frameworks such as the time of Carranza and the Mexican Revolution, the establishment of the Faculty of Anthropology at the National University, or the references to the implementation of Article Three of the 1917 Mexican Constitution. Yet these moments of *ladino* history give way to a dimension of myth from the outset, the realm established for the indigenous from the epigraph on. The eternal present in which yesterday, today, and tomorrow coexist indistinguishably is where these characters seem to be relegated to function—in clear opposition to those in control of measuring, dividing, and categorizing that historical continuum. Doctor Salazar, man of science, collector of watches, and sporadic practitioner of medicine at a rural clinic, leaves us with no doubts when he reveals that he needs to be reassured of the existence of the "real" world by winding all his watches at once and listening to them tick, for in his daily routine he deals only with those who live in the realm of the timeless. Since it is supposed that they have experienced no changes in their lives since time immemorial when the companion spirits led the Bolometic community out of the green meadows and into the gray mountains, far away from the invading white civilization, the indigenous peoples seem merely to relive their ancient narratives in the twentieth century. Even in their internal monologues on which Castellanos eavesdrops, these individual human beings with names and faces, laudable qualities as well as weaknesses, only recover the power of language to merge back into the narrative stream of traditional myth; they do not "curse the colonizer" as the appropriation of this privileged voice has been termed today. The predicament created by the linguistic silencing of the Amerindians (their economic oppression and cultural disappearance) has a correlative in Castellanos' need to find a narrative language with which to represent women's subjective voice as well. The translation of these stories allows the English language reader to discover what choices the author made for her characters to express their ideas, and what options she chose as vehicles for her own thoughts.

Throughout *City of Kings* the reader is constantly kept aware of the paradoxical nature of a national quest for some type of "modernity" imposed from above or outside. With its own cult figures and new myths—capitalism, education, Coca Cola, the media—grafted on or substituted for the old, the social and ethnic stratification of Mexican society still continues and the victimization (sacrifice) of the Indian is perpetuated in yet another guise: as tourist attraction, exploited laborer, or invisible national "treasure." At a critical time when this problem is being confronted in Mexico—as well as in the U.S. and around the world—yet again, Castellanos' stories are almost chilling in their thirty year old reminders to us all. The issue of the writer as witness to and mediator of cultural encounters is an extremely difficult role that can sometimes only forge between these groups something akin to what the title of the second story hints at: a fragile "truce," a relationship of inequality as yet unresolved. This space of opposition is the universe Rosario Castellanos inhabits. No one should miss out on the opportunity to experience her working at this challenge, for we can learn as much about our own culture as we do of others from her texts. This timely translation of *City of Kings* offers us that chance.

Claudia Schaefer
University of Rochester

Death of the Tiger

The Bolometic community was made up of families of the same lineage. Their protecting spirit, their *waigel*, was the tiger, whose name it was their right to brandish because of their bravery and their boldness.

After immemorial wanderings (fleeing from the coast, from the ocean and its suicidal temptation), the men of that race settled in the mountainous region of Chiapas, in a valley rich with meadowlands, groves, and springs. There, prosperity made them hold their heads high and made their spirits proud and ferocious. Many times the Bolometic went down to feast on the possessions of nearby tribes.

With the arrival of the white men—the *caxlanes*—the bellicose passion of the Bolometic was hurled into battle with a force that, as it clashed against the invaders' iron, ended in a crushing fall. Worse than conquered, paralyzed, the Bolometic felt deep within their very being the harshness of defeat, never before suffered. They were despoiled of their land, subjected to imprisonment and to slavery. The ones who managed to flee (their impoverished condition whispered this idea to them, made them invisible to the anger of their persecutors so they could carry it out) sought refuge in the mountains. There, they stopped to take account of what had been salvaged from the catastrophe. There, they began a precarious life in which the memory of past greatness became hazy, in which their history became a tame ember that no one could rekindle.

From time to time the bravest of the men went down to the neighboring lands to barter the produce of their harvest and visit the sacred places, calling upon the great powers to stop tormenting their *waigel* the tiger, for the *brujos* could hear it roaring, wounded, in the thicket of the mountains. The Bolometic were generous in their offerings, yet their pleas could not be heeded. The tiger would still have to receive many more wounds.

Because the greed of the *caxlanes* is not placated with predation, nor with tribute. It does not sleep. It lies awake in them, and their children, and their children's children. And the *caxlanes* moved forward, wide awake, trampling the earth with the iron hooves of their horses, casting everywhere their hawkeye, nervously cracking their whip.

The Bolometic saw the threat coming closer, but they did not run, as before, to take up weapons they no longer had the courage to wield. They huddled together, trembling with fear, in order to examine their conduct, as though they were about to appear before a demanding tribunal with no chance to appeal. They were not going to defend themselves; how could they if they had forgotten the art of battle, and had not yet learned that of argument? They were going to humble themselves. But the heart of the white man, of the *ladino*, is made of a material that pleas cannot soften. And clemency shines brighter in the helmet that adorns a captain's armor, than in the grains of sand that dot the writings of a clerk.

"The truth is consigned in this paper that speaks. And the truth is that all this land, with its slopes so good for sowing wheat, with its pine groves to cut down so there will be enough firewood and charcoal, with its rivers that will turn mills, all this is the property of Don Diego Mijangos y Orantes, who has proven his direct descendance from that other Don Diego Mijangos the conquistador, and from the Mijangos who came after him who were *encomenderos*. And that is why you, Sebastián Gómez Escopeta, and you, Lorenzo Pérez Diezmo, and you, Juan Domínguez Ventana, or whatever your name is, you're trespassing. You're squatting on land that doesn't belong to you, and that is a crime prosecuted by the law. Let's go, let's go, *chamulas*. Get out of here."

Centuries of submission had deformed the race. They quickly lowered their heads as a sign of obeisance: docilely, they turned their backs and departed. The women went first, carrying the children and the most indispensable household goods. The old ones, with their halting feet, were next. And in the rear, protecting the emigrants, the men.

Hard days of traveling, with no fixed destination. Abandoning one site as uninhabitable, and another so as not to quarrel with its owners. Their food and provisions grew scarce. Those most cruelly attacked by hunger dared to make nighttime pillages near the maize fields, taking advantage of the darkness to seize an ear of corn in season, the leaves of some vegetables. But the dogs picked up the scent of the stranger's presence and barked out their accusation. The guards came, brandishing machetes, and they raised such a cry that the intruder would flee in terror. Away he went, hungry, furtive, with his long hirsute hair and his clothing in shreds.

Hardship decimated the tribe. Ill protected from bad weather, the cold cast its lethal vapor upon them, and gradually shrouded them in a dense, whitish mist. First, the children died, without comprehending why, their little fists clenched tightly as if to hold on to the last shred of warmth. The old ones died, curled up next to the ashes of the dying embers, without a word of complaint. The women went into hiding to die, in a final gesture of pudency, just as they had hidden themselves to give birth in happier times.

Those were the ones who stayed behind, who would not live to see their new country. The village settled high up on a terraced slope, so high that it split the heart of the *caxlán* in two, even with its hardness. Blasted by hostile winds, poor, disdained by even the lowest, most vile forms of vegetation, the earth revealed the sterility of its belly in deep crevices. And water, of a poor quality, was far off.

Some stole pregnant ewes and grazed them secretly. The women set up looms, and waited for the first sheep to be shorn. Others plowed the land, this untamed, avaricious land. The rest set out on journeys to places consecrated for worship, to petition for divine benevolence.

But the years came in grimly, and hunger wandered freely from house to house, knocking on all doors with its bony hand.

The men, meeting in council, decided to leave. Their wives refused to eat the last mouthful of food, so as not to send them off empty-handed. And at the crossroads where the paths divide, they bid each other farewell.

Walking. Walking. The Bolometic did not rest at night. Their torchlights could be seen snaking through the darkness of the hills.

They reached Ciudad Real panting, their torn clothing sticky with sweat. The encrusted mud which had dried many days before now began to crack slowly, revealing their bare legs.

In Ciudad Real men no longer live according to whim, or simply to serve necessity. In the planning of this town of *caxlanes*, intelligence had predominated. The streets intersect geometrically. The houses are all of the same size, of a homogeneous style. Some display on their facades a noble coat of arms. Their owners are the descendants of those men skilled in war (the "conquistadors", the first colonizers) whose deeds still resound, lending a heroic resonance to certain family names: Marín, De la Tovilla, Mazariegos.

During the centuries of the colonial period and the first years of Independence, Ciudad Real was the seat of government of the province. It assumed the opulence and abundance of commerce; it spread the light of culture. But now, all that remained was the See of the upper ecclesiastical hierarchy: the Bishop's office.

Because the splendor of Ciudad Real now belonged only to memory. Ruin ate its heart out first. People without daring, without initiative, content with their heraldry, sunk in contemplation of their past, let go the staff of political power, abandoned the reins of commercial enterprise, closed the book on intellectual disciplines. Surrounded by a tight ring of silently hostile indigenous communities, the relationship Ciudad Real always maintained with them was ruled by injustice. Along with systematic plunder came a latent state of protest that several times had culminated in bloody uprisings; each time Ciudad Real was less able to restore calm alone. Neighboring towns—Comitán and Tuxtla, Chiapa de Corzo—came to its aid. Wealth, fame, and power shifted over to them. Ciudad Real was now nothing but a vain, empty shell, a scarecrow effective only on the spirit of the Indians, stubbornly clinging to terror.

The Bolometic crossed their first city streets to the tacit disapproval of the passers-by who, grimacing with affected prudishness, shunned any contact with such offensive misery.

The Indians, uncomprehending, insistent, curious, examined the spectacle laid before their eyes. The solid construction of the churches oppressed them, as if they were obligated to carry them on their backs. The exquisiteness of the ornamentation—some iron gratings, the detailed working of certain stones—aroused a desire to smash them. They laughed at the sudden appearance of objects whose use they could not even begin to imagine: fans, porcelain figurines, lace garments. They grew ecstatic before the photographer's display of his skill: postcards on which a melancholy young lady appears, meditating, next to a truncated column, while off in the distant horizon, the sun dies melancholically too.

And the people? How did the Bolometic view the people? They did not see the insignificance of these little men, short, fat, and ruddy, the dregs of an energetic, bold race. All that shone resplendently before their eyes was the streak of light that, in another time, had destroyed them. And through the ugliness, through the decadence of the present, the superstition of the conquered still glimpsed the mysterious signs of omnipotence of the god *caxlán*.

The women of Ciudad Real, the "*coletas*", slipped by with their tiny, reticent, dove-like steps; their eyes lowered, their cheeks reddened by the rough caress of the north wind. Mourning, silence, went with them. And when they spoke, they spoke with that mossy voice that lulls newborn babies to sleep, that consoles the sick, that attends to the dying. That voice of someone who watches men pass by through a case of glass.

The market place attracted the strangers with its bustle. Here is the place of abundance. Here, the corn that smothers the granaries with its golden yellow; here the red-blooded beasts, quartered, hanging from enormous hooks. Fleshy, succulent fruit: the peach with its ever young skin; vigorous, *macho* bananas; the apple that, in its acidic edge, carries the taste of a knife. And the coffee with its persuasive powers, that calls out from far away with its smell. And the baroque sweets, baptized with tribal, distant names: *tartaritas*, *africanos*. And the bread, with which God greets men every morning.

This is what the Bolometic saw, and they saw it with an astonishment that no longer held any greed, that precluded all desire for possession. With a sense of religious awe.

The gendarme in charge of watching that area was walking among the stands, distracted, humming a little tune, brushing away an occasional fly. But when he noticed the presence of those ragged vagabonds (he was accustomed to seeing them, but one at a time, not in a group the way they were now, without any *ladino* in charge) he automatically assumed a guarded stance. He gripped his stick more tightly, ready to use it at the first attempt at robbery or at violating that long, nebulous clause of a law that he had never read, but whose existence he suspected: disturbing the peace. Nonetheless, the Bolometic's intentions seemed to be peaceful. They had left the stands to go look for an empty place on the steps of the Church of la Merced. Squatting down, the Indians patiently picked the lice out of their hair and ate them. The gendarme watched them from a distance with satisfaction, because it was his role to be disdainful.

A man who was following the Bolometic finally decided to approach them. Chubby, bald, animated with a false joviality, he spoke to them in their dialect:

"*Yday*, *chamulas*? Are you looking for a job?"

The Bolometic exchanged quick, suspicious glances. Each of them left the responsibility for answering to the next. Finally the one who seemed most respectable (and was most respected because of his age and because he had made an earlier trip to Ciudad Real), asked:

"Is there some possibility that you can give us work? Are you, by any chance, a hirer?"

"Exactly. And I'm known for my honesty. My name is Juvencio Ortiz."

"Oh, yes. Don Juvencio."

The comment was more a sign of courtesy than an echo of his reputation. Silence spread between the two speakers like a stain. Don Juvencio tapped on the bulge of his stomach, at the height where his gold watch chain should have been looped on the button of his vest. Finding that he was not yet the owner of a watch chain made him spur on the conversation.

"So then? Shall we make a deal?"

But the Indians were in no hurry. There is never any hurry to fall into a trap.

"We came down from our territory. There's very little food there, *patrón*. The crops won't grow."

"All the more in my favor, *chamulas*. Let's step into my office and finalize the details."

Don Juvencio started walking, certain that the Indians would follow. Hypnotized by his air of absolute confidence, the Bolometic trailed along behind him.

What Don Juvencio called, with so much pomp, his office, was nothing more than a tiny cubbyhole, a little booth on one of the streets running parallel to the one where the market place was located. The furniture consisted of two pine tables (on more than one occasion the splinters on their badly sanded tops had torn the sleeves of the only suits Don Juvencio and his associate owned), a shelf overflowing with papers, and two unstable chairs. Perched on one of them, with all the tentativeness of a bird, was Don Juvencio's associate: a long profile hidden by a green plastic visor. He cackled when he saw the newcomers:

"Did you get anything good, Don Juvencio?"

"What was available, your honor. The competition is rough. Hirers with less credentials—I hold the title of lawyer, issued by the School of Law of Ciudad Real!—and with less experience than I have, are making off with my clients."

"They use other means. You never wanted to resort to alcohol. A drunk Indian certainly doesn't know what he's doing or what he's committing himself to. But just to save yourself the price of a drink..."

"It's not that. It's just that taking advantage of the ignorance of these poor people is, as his Excellency, Don Manuel Oropeza says, a mean trick."

Don Juvencio's associate bared his teeth with a malicious little laugh.

"Well, you see where your ideas are leading us to. You were the one who swore that everything else could disappear from this world but that there would always be enough Indians to go around. And now we're finding out the truth. The plantations that put us in charge of their management are in danger of losing their harvests because of a lack of hired hands."

"Wise men know when to change their minds, my dear partner. I also said... but, anyway, there's no reason to complain now. Here they are, right before your eyes."

Don Juvencio made the pompous gesture of a magician drawing aside the curtain to reveal some wondrous trick. But his associate's sense of appreciation remained unmoved.

"You mean these...?!"

Don Juvencio found himself in the painful position of imitating his voice:

"You mean these! What kind of a tone is that, your grace! What's wrong with them?"

Don Juvencio's associate shrugged.

"As the saying goes, they've already got one foot in the grave. They won't be able to survive the climate on the coast. And since you're so scrupulous..."

Don Juvencio went up to his associate, humorously raising a threatening finger.

"Ah, you sly old fox! No wonder they call you a bringer of bad tidings. But keep in mind, your lordship, the old saying that advises us not to get involved in things that aren't our concern. Do you really think we're responsible if these Indians can stand the climate or not? Our job is to make sure that they show up alive in front of the plantation owner. What happens afterward is none of our business."

And to avoid any further discussion, he went over to the shelf and pulled out a sheaf of papers. After giving them to his partner, Don

Juvencio turned to the Bolometic and said sternly:

"All right, *chamulas*, get in line. Go on over to the gentleman's table one at a time, and answer his questions. And no lying, *chamulas*, because that man is a *brujo*, and he can bring you harm. Do you know why he wears that visor? So that the power of his eyes won't hurt you."

The Bolometic listened to this warning with increasing apprehension. How would they be able to go on concealing their true name? They surrendered it—they put their *waigel*, their wounded tiger, in the power of those hands stained with ink.

"Pablo Gómez Bolom."

"Daniel Hernández Bolom."

"José Domínguez Bolom."

The eyes of Don Juvencio's associate bore into the Indians with needless suspicion. They were pulling his leg, as usual. Later, when they escaped from the plantations without paying their debts, no one would be able to find them. Because the village they said they were from didn't exist, and the names they claimed as theirs were false.

But no, by the Holy Virgin of Mercy, this time he'd had enough! Don Juvencio's partner pounded his fist on the table, ready to explode. Except his knowledge of the native tongue wasn't good enough to let him get into an argument. Grumbling to himself, he shot out:

"Bolom! I'm going to bolom you and teach you a lesson. All right, next."

When he had finished, he told Don Juvencio:

"There are forty of them. What plantation are we going to send them to?"

"We'll shut up don Federico Werner, the one who's been hounding us the most. Write this down: 'El Suspiro' coffee plantation, Tapachula."

While he was writing, his eyes protected by the green visor, Don Juvencio's partner poked at the wound:

"There aren't enough."

"What do you mean, there aren't enough? Forty Indians to bring in the coffee harvest for one plantation, and that's not enough? It's better than nothing."

"Not all forty of them are going to make it. They won't even be able to stand the trip there."

And Don Juvencio's partner turned the page, certain that he was right.

With the advance money they received, the Bolometic started out on their journey. As they left behind the harshness of the mountains, they were overcome more and more by a tepid, lethargic air that broke their staunch asceticism. In this air, sweetened with mixed aromas, they smelled delight. And they were startled, like a bloodhound who is given an unknown prey to track down.

As the heights abandoned them so brusquely, their eardrums burst. They ached, they festered. When the Bolometic reached the sea, they believed its great fury to be mute.

The only presence that never left them was the cold. It would not give up the stronghold where it had always been master. Every day, always at the same hour, even if the tropical sun could have melted stone, the cold uncoiled like an ugly snake and slithered through the bodies of the Bolometic, locking their jaws and their bodies in a terrible convulsion. After it came to visit, the bodies of the Bolometic were left as though dead; they began to shrink, bit by bit, to fit into the grave.

The survivors of that long summer could never return. Their debts added link upon link, and chained them down. In the scar of their eardrums echoed, more weakly every time, the voices of the women calling out to them, the voices of their children fading away.

The tiger in the mountain was never heard of again.

The Truce

Rominka Pérez Taquibequet, from the region of Mukenjá, was walking along with her sloshing jug, just filled with water. A woman like all the others of her tribe, an ageless stone; silent and erect to keep the weight of her burden balanced. Each time her body swayed as she climbed the steep path from the arroyo to her hut, the pounding of her blood hammered at her temples, at the tips of her fingers. Fatigue. And a vapor of illness, of delirium, clouding over her eyes. It was two o'clock in the afternoon.

At a bend in the road, without a sound to announce his presence, a man appeared. His boots were spattered with mud, his shirt dirty, torn to shreds; his beard showed several weeks' growth.

Rominka stopped in front of him, stunned by surprise. From the white color (or was it extreme paleness?) of his face, it was easy to tell that the stranger was a *caxlán*. But by what roads had he come? What was he looking for in such a remote place? Now, with his long, fine hands, on which the harsh weather had vented its anger, he was making gestures that Rominka was unable to interpret. And to her timid but insistent questions, the intruder responded not with words, but with a pained rattling in his throat.

The wind fled into the heights, shrieking mournfully. A washed-out, cold sun shot its arrows down upon that barren hill. Not one cloud. Down below, the childlike gurgling of the water, and there the two of them, motionless with the anguished weight of a bad dream.

Rominka was brought up to know about this. The one who walks on another's land, borrowed land, steals the air when he breathes. Because things (all things, the things we see, and also the things we use) do not belong to us. They have another master. And the master punishes when someone takes over a place, a tree, even a name.

The master, the *pukuj*—no one would know how to invoke him if the *brujos* had not shared their revelation—is a spirit. Invisible, he comes and goes, listening to the desires in the heart of man. And when he wants to do harm he turns the hearts of some against others, he twists friendships, sparks wars. Or he dries up the insides of child-bearing women, of those who create life. Or he says "hunger", and every mouthful of food turns to ashes in the mouths of the hungry.

In past times, as the old ones with long memories tell it, some men unhappy with the way the *pukuj* kept them under subjection contrived a scheme to take away his strength. They gathered tribute in a net: *posol*, seeds, eggs. They set it at the entrance of the cave where the *pukuj* sleeps. And next to the provisions was a vessel of *posh*, of firewater.

When the *pukuj* fell asleep, his limbs weak from drunkenness, the men threw themselves upon him and bound him hand and foot with thick ropes. The prisoner's howls made the mountains tremble down to their roots. Threats, promises, nothing got him his freedom until one of the men standing guard (out of fear, out of respect, who knows?) cut his bonds. Since then the *pukuj* has roamed free, appearing sometimes in the form of an animal, sometimes dressed as a *ladino*. And woe upon the one who meets up with him; he stands marked before the tribe, and for all time. In his trembling hands, unable to grasp objects; in his cheeks drained of blood; in his perpetually startled, frenzied eyes, the others recognize his terrible adventure. His relatives, his friends, gather around to defend him. It is useless. Before their eyes, the marked one turns his back on sanity, on life. The spoils of the *pukuj* are the cadavers of children and young people, and the madmen.

But Rominka did not want to die, did not want to go mad. Her children, still babbling, were crying out for her. Her husband loved her. And her own flesh, even if dried-up or sick, was alive, and shuddered with terror at the threat.

It was of no use, Rominka knew only too well, of no use to run away. The *pukuj* is here and there, and no shadow will hide us from its pursuit. But if we throw ourselves upon its mercy?

The woman fell to her knees. After she put the jug on the ground, she pleaded:

"Master of the mountain, have pity on me!"

She did not dare to search the apparition's face. But imagining its' expression to be hostile, she continued pleading feverishly. And little by little, without really understanding why herself, she began slipping from pleas into confessions. Things she had told no one, not even herself, gushed out like a stream of pus from a squeezed boil. Hatreds that devastated her soul, cowardly compliance, secret lusts, thefts tenaciously denied. And then Rominka knew the reason why she, from among all, had been chosen to placate the gods' hunger for truth with her humiliation. Words rolled forth from her lips, as they should from every human lip, red with shame. And as Rominka pulled the crust off her sins, she cried. Because it hurts to be left naked. But at the price of this pain she was buying the good will of the apparition, the master of the mountains, the *pukuj*, so he would go back to live in the caves, so he would not come and upset people's lives.

However, something was still missing. Because the *pukuj*, not content with what he had been given, shoved Rominka brutally. With a shriek of anguish, and using the jug to shield herself, she ran toward the small village, stirring up a flutter of chickens, a yapping of dogs, cries of alarm from the children.

The man followed her, a short distance behind, panting, almost at the point of collapse from the effort. He was waving his hands in the air, he was saying something. One more yell, and Rominka fell down at the door of her house. Water spilled out from the overturned jug. And before the dogs could lick it up, before the earth could swallow it, the man fell headlong onto the puddle. Because he was thirsty.

The women had withdrawn to the back of their huts, holding their babies close to the breast. A small boy ran to the maize field to call the men.

Not all of them were there. The furrowed ground they bent over was poor. Exhausted from giving all that its poor body had, it now yielded only pitiful spikes of corn, grain without substance. And so, many Indians had begun looking to other means for their sustenance. Violating their own customs and the laws of the *ladinos*, the men from Mukenjá were clandestinely distilling alcohol.

Time went by before the authorities became aware of this. No one notified them of the accidents the distillers had when a still exploded inside a hut. A conspiracy of silence shrouded the disasters. And the wounded, howling with pain, vanished into the mountain.

But the businessmen, the merchants from Custital established as leaders of the municipality of Chamula, soon noticed that something unusual was happening. Their stockpiles of alcohol did not sell out as rapidly as before, and now there was even a situation where bottles of liquor were warehoused for months upon end. Could the Indians have suddenly become abstinent? That idea was absurd. How would they celebrate their religious days, their civil ceremonies, the events of their everyday family life? Alcohol is indispensable in those rites. And the rites were still being observed with scrupulous attention, down to the final detail. The women were still weaning their children by giving them a rag soaked in *posh* to suck on.

With the double zeal of an authority tolerating no tricks and a supplier of firewater permitting no mischief, the Municipal Secretary of Chamula, Rodolfo López, ordered an inquiry to be made. He himself took charge of it. Imposing fines, as the law prescribed, seemed to him an ineffectual measure. They were dealing with Indians, not with intelligent people, and the punishment had to be severe. So they would learn, he said.

They scoured a large part of the area without success. Each time his mule slipped on those rocky plains, a greater and greater rage built up inside the Municipal Secretary. And each time that a thundershower soaked him through to the bone. And at every place where he became mired in the thick mud.

When he finally caught up with the guilty parties, in Mukenjá, Rodolfo López was trembling so that he could not clearly state their punishment. His subordinates thought they had misunderstood him. But the Secretary spoke without thinking about his own responsibility or the judgement of his superiors; they were too far away, they were not going to pay attention to matters of such little importance. The certainty of his impunity had fed his vengeance, and now vengeance was devouring him too. His flesh, his blood, his spirit, were no longer enough to withstand his desire to destroy, to punish. He repeated the instructions to his subordinates, making signs with his hands. Perhaps he didn't order them to set fire to the huts. But when the straw began to burn, and the walls creaked and those who were inside tried to flee, Rodolfo López made them go back, hitting them with the butt of his rifle. And with the desperation of a man who has almost choked to death, he breathed in the odor of roasting flesh.

The act took place in plain view of everyone. They all heard the screams, the crackling of matter as it succumbed to a greedier, more powerful element. The Municipal Secretary left that place certain that the example would stay in their thoughts. And that every time necessity presented them the temptation of clandestine acts, they would shun it in horror.

The Municipal Secretary was mistaken. Scarcely had a few months gone by when the demand for alcohol at his store again dropped off. With a resigned gesture, he sent government agents to carry out an investigation.

The agents wasted no time. They went directly to Mukenjá. They found small factories, and confiscated them. This time there were no deaths. It was enough for them to steal. Here, and in other villages. Because cruelty seemed to multiply the guilty parties, whose spirit, degraded by misfortune, gave itself over to punishment with a sort of fascination.

When the boy had finished talking (he was breathless from running and because of the importance of the news he had to tell), the men of Mukenjá looked at each other in confusion. Only someone endowed with the supernatural powers of the *pukuj*, or with the fury and the precision of a government agent seizing his prey, could climb hills as inaccessible as these.

Either of the two possibilities was inevitable, and to try to avoid or postpone it by attempting to run away was wasted effort. The men of Mukenjá faced the situation without even thinking about their farm instruments as weapons of defense. Unarmed, they returned to the village.

The *caxlán* was there, lying on the ground, his face dripping with water. He was not asleep. But the hoarse sound of death was constricting his breathing. He tried to stand when he saw the Indians approaching, but could only lift himself up halfway, and was unable to hold that position. His cheek smashed silently into the mud.

The display of another's weakness made the Indians wild. They came prepared to endure violence, and the relief of finding no threat was quickly replaced with rage, an irrational rage that sought its basis and its justification through action.

Jumpy, the men moved from one spot to another, asking for details about the stranger's arrival. Rominka told of her encounter with him. It was an incoherent tale in which the repetition of the word *pukuj*, and the tears and the terrible anguish of the narrator, gave that still-amorphous frenzy a form to pour into.

Pukuj. Because of the evil influence of the one who lay here at their feet, there were never enough crops, the *brujos* ate away the flocks, illnesses would not leave them alone. The Indians had tried in vain to ingratiate themselves with the dark powers of the *pukuj* by means of offerings and sacrifices. The *pukuj* continued to choose his victims. And now, impelled by who knows what necessity, by who knows what greed, it had abandoned its den, and disguised as a *ladino* it walked the mountain ridges, it lay in wait for travelers.

One of the old ones drew closer. He asked the fallen man what was the cause of his suffering, and what he had come to demand of them. The fallen man did not answer.

The men looked around for what they could find readily at hand for the attack: cudgels, stones, machetes. One woman, with a smoking incensory, made several turns around the fallen man, tracing out a magic circle from which he could no longer escape.

Then they unleashed their fury. Cudgel that pounds, stone that crushes the skull, machete that severs limbs. The women shouted from behind the walls of the huts, inciting the men to finish off their criminal work.

When it was finished the dogs came over to lick up the spilt blood. Later the buzzards came down.

The frenzy was drawn out artificially with drink. Long into the night, melancholy cries still echoed over the hills.

The following day they all returned to their usual labors. A slight dryness of the mouth, weakness of the muscles, clumsiness of the tongue, were the only reminders of the events of the previous day. And the sensation that they had freed themselves from an evil spell, had rid themselves of an unbearable weight.

But the truce was not a lasting one. There were new malignant spirits infesting the air. And that year the harvest at Mukenjá was as scarce as before. The *brujos*, devourers of beasts, devourers of men, demanded food. Illnesses too were decimating them. It was necessary to kill again.

Aceite guapo

As he dug holes to plant corn on the hillside of Yalcuc, Daniel Castellanos Lampoy paused, exhausted. Weariness was always with him now. His strength was gone, and, like now, his work was left unfinished.

Resting beside a tree, Daniel muttered to himself, bitterly foreseeing another lean year of bad harvests and thinking up excuses to satisfy the landowner to whom he would still be in debt. But he didn't stop to consider the real cause of his problems: he had grown old.

It had taken him awhile to realize it. How was he to notice that time was going by, when its passing had brought him nothing? Neither a family, which had scattered when his wife died, nor the fruits of his labor, nor a position of honor among the people of his tribe. Now, Daniel was just like he had started out: empty-handed. But he was old and had to admit it. The proof was in the glances other people gave him, grim with suspicion, quick with alarm, heavy with disapproval.

Daniel knew what those glances meant: he too had looked at others the same way in the past. They meant that if death had not taken a man this old, it was because he had made a pact with darker forces, because he had agreed to become a spy and an instrument for their evil intentions.

An old man is not the same thing as a *brujo*. He is not a man who knows what brings harm and how to avoid it; he is not a force that bends with the bribes of those who entreat it, or knowledge sold at some agreeable price. Nor is he a sign that sometimes changes into its opposite and may be favorable.

No, an old man is evil incarnate, and no one should go looking to him for compassion, for that would be useless. He need only sit at the side of the road or at the door to his house, and whatever he contemplates will be transformed into bare land, into ruin, into death. Neither pleas nor gifts do any good. His mere presence will bring harm. One must stay far away from him, avoid him; let him be consumed by hunger and need, lie in wait in the shadows to end to his life with the stroke of a machete, incite a crowd to stone him to death.

An old man's family, if he has one, does not dare to defend him. The family itself is constrained by fear, anxious to put an end to the anguish and the risks brought by contact with the supernatural.

Daniel Castellanos Lampoy realized, all of a sudden, the future that awaited him. And he was afraid. At night, his eyes would not close with sleep, but remained wide open to the horror of his situation, and to the urgency of finding an escape.

Imperceptibly, Daniel withdrew from everyone. He no longer went to the plaza on market days, for he was afraid of meeting someone who would later attribute to that meeting a fall on the road, a sudden illness, the loss of an animal from his herd.

But the very act of keeping to himself ended up making him more suspicious. Why was he shutting himself off? Undoubtedly to conjure up illnesses, breakdowns, misfortunes that others would suffer later on.

It isn't easy to wipe away the stigma of old age. People remember: when I was a child, Daniel Castellanos Lampoy was already a mature man. Now that mature man is me. How many years must have gone by?

The number doesn't matter. What matters are the wrinkles in the skin, the hunching of the back, the weakness of the body, and the gray hairs, whose very strangeness is just one more sign of a predestined fate. And those eyes, whose opacity hides the power to annihilate.

Where could he go to find refuge from the unwavering, implacable persecution of the tribe? Instinctively, Daniel thought of the Church: no one would dare come to kill him at the altar of the protective deities.

Yes, what Daniel needed to do was become a *martoma*, the steward of some saint in the Church of San Juan, in Chamula.

There would be difficulties in carrying out his plan, and Daniel was not unaware of them. What merits could he present to those in charge? His past experience didn't even include a civil position, much less a religious one. He couldn't boast any title of "former authority" and besides, now he was already marked by decrepitude. But nevertheless, Daniel would have to convince everyone with the fervor of his petitions, the humbleness of his pleas, the abundance of his gifts.

But Daniel was not eloquent. For years, the years since he had become a widower, since his children had gone, since he had been all alone, he had spoken to no one. Little by little he had begun to forget the meaning of words; the names of many objects no longer came to mind. In order to weave together a phrase, it was a terrible struggle for him to find the proper sounds, and then he was not able to express himself clearly or fluently. When he felt the attention of others centered upon him in conversation, a sudden rush of blood invaded his throat, and he could only end with a painful stammer. How could he appear before the assembly, and how was he ever going to defend his desire for a position? His only remaining chance for success was through bribery.

Daniel Castellanos Lampoy unearthed his money jar so that he could count its contents. Incredulous, he passed the coins between his hands, over and over again. He had always been sure there were more, and now, when he saw how few they were and how little they amounted to, he couldn't overcome his astonishment.

Finally, he took a road he knew very well: the one leading to the "El Rosario" hacienda, where he was an indentured peon.

Don Gonzalo Urbina saw him coming with a sense of mistrust, and before he could begin to explain the purpose of his visit, cut him short by asking for payment of back debts. Daniel had to resign himself to placating the demands of the *caxlán*, promising to be more punctual in the future, but no longer had an opportunity to ask for the loan he needed so badly.

Don Gonzalo listened to Daniel's protests with an expression of feigned severity. In his heart he was pleased. From the beginning he had sensed the question of a loan, and had slyly avoided it. He felt sorry for this poor Indian who didn't even have a pot to piss in, and whose children, for years, had refused to pay the debts he ran up. He felt sorry for him, but what would happen to his business if he started handing out favors? Obligations first, and then charity, damn it all.

Daniel went back to his hut, feeling completely dejected. Now who could he turn to for help? He thought about the hirers of Ciudad Real, but he quickly got rid of that idea. No hirer would employ a man in his condition to work the fields of an estate. Three years earlier, when he wanted to go to the coast to put together a few *centavos*, they had refused to take him. They wanted younger men, men who could withstand the rigors of the climate and the harshness of the work.

But what the day kept hidden from him, insomnia revealed: a plan he would propose to Don Juvencio Ortiz.

Don Juvencio, the hirer, thought highly of Daniel Castellanos because he was a man of his word. His sweat had made money for him before on the estates, when he wasn't so old; he had gotten good recommendations from the bosses. Don Juvencio would give credence to his words. He would fool him by promising that the one to be hired would not be him, but one of his sons... or perhaps both of them. He would ask for an advance, and then take off. Who was going to find him if he left his village? Besides, no one would be interested in looking for him, it was his sons they would go after. They were the ones who would have been contracted, and whose pictures the authorities would have. If the prosecutors found them and made them go to work on the estates, Daniel would be pleased. A just punishment for the way they had left him, abandoned, all these years; a just punishment for their ingratitude, for the hardness of their hearts.

Don Juvencio did not distrust Daniel's words. He remembered this Indian who, in his good years, had been a responsible peon; he knew his children too, but something made him stroke his chin in thought. Hadn't he heard that they had become estranged from their father? Daniel denied it, vehemently. The proof that it wasn't true was right there in their pictures, and in the fact that they had asked him to make arrangements for them with the hirer, and that he was to pick up their advances. Not for just one, but for both of them, Daniel insisted.

"You know what will happen to you if you're lying to me, *chamulita*?"

Daniel nodded. He knew that Don Juvencio held the power of his true name, his *chulel*, and of the *waigel* of his tribe. He trembled for an instant, but then he recovered. At the altars of San Juan no threat would be able to touch him.

Don Juvencio Ortiz finally accepted, noting down the names of Daniel's sons in his books. He handed the money over to the old man, who set straight out on the road to Chamula.

There he learned about the steps he needed to follow in order to be named a *martoma*. He spoke with the sacristan of the church, Xaw Ramírez Paciencia, he attended public meetings of the leaders, and when he had the opportunity, he jangled the coins that he was carrying.

The others looked at him with a glimmer of mockery. In a man bent over with age, how had such an untimely ambition taken root? Poor old man, this would probably be his final dream.

In the meantime, Daniel put into practice all the sly tricks that his cunning could suggest. He began rising earlier than usual. When the sacristan, sleepy and disheveled, came down from the tower with his enormous keys in order to open the church doors, he found Daniel already there, waiting for him. He followed in right behind the sacristan, and he would kneel before any image, for hours at a time, praying confusedly out loud.

Daniel made so many fervent declarations of devotion that this, along with the expectation of the recompense they would receive from him, made the leaders decide to act on the old man's behalf. They granted him the honor of being the steward of Santa Margarita.

Now Daniel finally had someone to kneel down in front of, someone to be the object of his caretaking and his scrupulous attention. Now, finally, he had someone to talk to.

The fear that had pushed him violently to the feet of the saint gave way, little by little, to love. Daniel fell in love with the one who would be his final patron.

For hours he gazed in ecstasy at her figure, nearly invisible among the heap of rags draped over it. He made a trip to Jobel to buy showy flowered fabrics for her, tiny mirrors framed in celluloid, candles made of fine wax, handfuls of incense. And from the mountains he brought her garlands of flowers.

Daniel invited the other stewards to the ceremony of the changing of the saint's garments. They came and sat in front of the altar, in a well-swept space strewn with fragrant *juncia* plants, a jug full of liquor within reach.

With trembling respect, Daniel removed the pins that held up the cloth, and began to unwrap it. Carefully, he folded the first cloth. Then the stewards filled the drinking gourd with alcohol, and they drank. When the second cloth was folded they repeated their libation, and then did the same with the cloths that followed. Finally the saint shone in her nakedness, but no one was capable of contemplating her, for they had all gotten blind with drunkenness.

The dirty linens were exchanged for new ones, and then were taken down to the arroyo. There a ceremony was held to purify the springs, attended by all the stewards, with the liquor jug. While Daniel washed the cloths, the others awaited the moment when they would be invited to drink the soapy water that had cleansed the garments of Santa Margarita. To remove its bad taste and to assist them in swallowing it, they turned to the firewater. Drunkenness was part of the ritual, and they all gave themselves over to it without remorse, with the satisfaction of those who carry out their duty.

Daniel came to again after these celebrations and was suddenly gripped by great anguish. How much time did he have left under Santa Margarita's protective shadow? When his period of stewardship ended, he would go back into the storm, to the dangers of the outside world. And he didn't have the strength to confront that situation. He was very old, and so tired!

In the meantime, he continued to arrive at the church before anyone else. Xaw Ramírez Paciencia, the sacristan, watched him, intrigued, from the baptistery. How many hours will he last like that, down on his knees? And what is he doing? Is he praying? You can see his lips move. But even if you went up next to him you wouldn't be able to understand him. He doesn't look like a real *Tzotzil*. The *Tzotziles* have a different way of praying.

Daniel's words were not a prayer. They were something simpler: before his patron, he had "the gift of gab". Just ordinary matters, casual observations. How the rains were late; how a coyote was lurking around the chicken coops in San Juan, and last night it had a field day with Señora Xmel's chickens; how the assistant mayor was sick, and the healers hadn't been able to lay their finger on the cause.

Not one petition, not one reproach. Of course, the saint, like a child and the careless child she is, forgets her obligations. She leaves the world to its disorder, she forgets about those who have placed their trust in her. But Daniel prefers to thank her for her favors, and he ponders the harvest, the great harvest that the village of Yalcuc will bring in this year. And he marvels at the great number of male children who have been born lately to the families of his tribe. And he rejoices that almost all the men who went to harvest coffee along the coast (among them may be his own sons, who knows?) are returning safe and healthy from the plantations.

Daniel never talked about himself. What was there to say? He was old, and Santa Margarita wasn't going to enjoy tales of long ago. And no matter how hard he tried to remember, his memory mixed people up, it got places all turned around. What would the lady think? That Daniel was raving, that he was a liar, that he was dotty.

With these conversations and others, the candles that Daniel had brought in the early morning hours were burning out, the day was coming to an end. So quickly? And Daniel still hasn't said what he's been wanting to say. But he says good-bye, and promises to return tomorrow. Because now the sacristan, Xaw Ramírez Paciencia, is clanking the keys, the enormous keys to the main door, and that's the sign he is going to lock up.

As Daniel left, he was saying to himself: this won't go on past tomorrow. I'll tell my troubles to Santa Margarita, and I'll ask her for a miracle, the miracle that I won't have to go back to Yalcuc, that I will continue to be her steward for ever and ever.

But when tomorrow was today, a sort of timidity paralyzed the old man's tongue, and would not loosen it except to twaddle about other people, to stammer incoherent litanies.

One afternoon when he went to see the changing of the garments of San Agustín along with the other stewards, drunkenness dragged him, frantic, disheveled, gesticulating, up to the altar of his patron. He shouted at her, insisting that she protect him from the persecution of the people of his tribe, that she protect him from a shameful death, that she give him the means to remain here as a steward one more year, even if it were just one more year.

The following day Daniel had the confused feeling that his secret was no longer hidden from Santa Margarita. He went to her, hoping to find some sign of benevolence. But the saint remained immobile within her heavy garments, unmindful of what was taking place around her.

Daniel began speaking to her in a low voice, but his passion grew uncontrollably until he was howling, to the point where he was hitting his own head with clenched fists. He felt a hand on his shoulder, shaking him. It was the sacristan.

"What are you shouting for, *tatik*? No one can hear you."

Daniel heard this remonstration with the same sense of scandal with which one hears heresy. Did the sacristan, a man who prayed the mass for the saints during feast days, dare to maintain that the saints were nothing more than deaf, lifeless pieces of wood, with no hint of intelligence or goodness? But Xaw, anxious to display his knowledge, added:

"Look at Santa Margarita's face. It's white, it's *ladina*, the same as San Juan, as Santo Tomás, as all of them. She talks *Castilla*. How are you going to make her understand *Tzotzil*?"

Daniel stopped, astonished. Xaw was right. And from that moment he tried to remember the only words of Spanish he had ever spoken, back when he was on the plantations, when he dealt with the shop-keepers in Jobel. But no, they were useless. None of them expressed his desperation, his urgent need for help. Xaw again approached with advice.

"Do you want to talk Castilla, *martoma*? There's a potion good for that, I drink it when I really need to. It's called *aceite guapo*. The pharmacies in Jobel sell it. But you have to have cash, lots of cash. Because it's very expensive."

Daniel Castellanos Lampoy dipped into the alms that the faithful had given to his patron, and began his journey to the city.

He roamed around like a fool until he came to a drugstore where they heard his request. He waited patiently while everyone else was taken care of, even though he had been the first to arrive; he humbly endured the bad manners and sneers of the clerks; he accepted, without protest, their overcharging and then shortchanging him. But at the end of the day, Daniel returned to Chamula with a bottle of *aceite guapo* that would allow him to speak with Santa Margarita.

He waited until he was kneeling at the feet of his patron before he opened it. The flavor was disagreeable and strong, the effects very similar to those of alcohol. Under the influence of the drug, Daniel began to feel that everything was spinning around him. A festive mood came over him. He laughed wildly, thinking now that the dangers threatening him were false, remote, without any basis. He made fun of everyone because he felt stronger than any man, and young and free and happy. Out there, through the haze surrounding Santa Margarita, he thought he glimpsed a wink of complicity that made him even crazier.

Xaw laughed also, from a distance. But not everyone found the spectacle equally amusing. The *martomas* were angry that one of their group would violate custom and give himself over to solitary drunkenness with no reason, thus staining the dignity of their position and the respect due to the church.

The following day Daniel Castellanos Lampoy's senses were so deadened that he didn't notice the hostile atmosphere now surrounding him.

The third time that he became intoxicated with the miraculous liquor, the *martomas*, gathered in council, decided to relieve that indecent old man of his responsibilities, and throw him bodily out of the church.

Xaw could do nothing on his behalf, and Daniel slept off his last drunk in the open fields.

A merciful unconsciousness enveloped him. For a few more hours, fear would not freeze his blood; it would not make him flee without direction from an unknown pursuer and an inexorable destiny.

The Luck of Teodoro Méndez Acúbal

Walking along the streets of Jobel (with his eyes lowered, as befitted his humble station), Teodoro Méndez Acúbal found a coin. Half covered by the trash on the ground, filthy with mud, dulled from use, it had gone unnoticed by the *caxlanes*. Because the *caxlanes* walk with their heads held high out of pride, mindful even from a distance of the important business demanding their attention.

Teodoro stopped, more in disbelief than from greed. Kneeling down, pretending to tie the cords of one of his sandals, he waited until he was certain that no one was watching him before he picked up his discovery. Quickly, he slipped it between the layers of his sash.

He stood up again, swaying, for a sort of dizziness had come over him: weakness in the joints, dryness of the mouth, his vision clouded, as if his heart were beating right in the middle of his forehead.

Staggering from one side to another like a drunk, Teodoro began walking. On more than one occasion, passers-by pushed him out of the way to keep him from knocking them over. But Teodoro's thoughts were too agitated to notice what was happening around him. The coin, hidden in the folds of his sash, had changed him into a different man. A stronger man than before, that's true. But also a more fearful one.

He turned slightly off the footpath he was following back to his village and sat down at the trunk of a tree. What if it had all been nothing but a dream? Pale with anxiety, Teodoro's hands went up to his sash. Yes, there, hard and round, was the coin. Teodoro unwrapped it, he moistened it with his breath and with saliva, he rubbed it against his clothing. On the surface of the metal (silver for sure, judging from its whitish color) the outline of a profile appeared. Proud. And around it, letters, numbers, signs. Weighing it in his hands, biting it, making it ring, Teodoro finally was able to figure its value.

So now, by a stroke of luck, he had become rich. Richer than if he owned a flock of sheep, richer than if he had an enormous field of maize. He was as rich as... as a *caxlán*. And Teodoro was astonished that the color of his skin remained the same.

Images of his family members (his wife, his three children, his elderly parents) tried to insinuate themselves into Teodoro's dream world. But he brushed them aside with a gesture of displeasure. He wasn't obligated to include anyone in his discovery, much less to share it. He worked to keep the household going. That was right, it was normal, it's a man's duty. But anything else, like luck, was his. Exclusively his.

So when Teodoro reached his hut and sat down by the embers to eat, he said nothing. His silence made him feel ashamed, as if by keeping quiet he was mocking the others. And like a punishment there grew, alongside his shame, a feeling of loneliness. Teodoro was a man set apart, silenced by a secret. And he agonized with physical sickness, cramps in his stomach, chills inside his bones. Why suffer like this? All he had to do was say one word, and the pain would go away. To keep himself from speaking it aloud, Teodoro touched, through the weave of his sash, the bulge made by the metal.

At night, lying awake, he said to himself: what shall I buy? Because until now he never had any desire to own things. He was so convinced that they had nothing to do with him that he passed them by without curiosity, without greed. And now he wasn't going to get into thinking about things they needed—blankets, machetes, hats. No. You buy those things with what you earn. But Méndez Acúbal had not earned this coin. His luck had brought it, it was a gift. It was given to him so he could to play with it, so he could lose it, so he could provide himself with something useless and beautiful.

Teodoro didn't know a thing about prices. Beginning with his next trip to Jobel, he began to pay attention to the dealings between buyers and sellers. They both seemed to stay calm. One of them affecting, perhaps, a lack of interest, and the other a desire to please, they talked about *reales*, about *tostones*, about pounds, about yards. And even about more things that spun around dizzily in Teodoro's head, without letting him catch hold of them.

Exhausted, Teodoro decided not to continue debating any longer, and abandoned himself to the delicious thought that in exchange for the silver coin he could have anything at all he wanted.

Months passed before Méndez Acúbal made his final, irrevocable decision. It was a paste figure, a little statue of the Virgin. It was also a real discovery, because the figure lay among a pile of objects that decorated a store window. From that moment on, Teodoro began hovering near it like a lover. Hour after hour would pass by. And there he was, always, like a sentinel, next to the window glass.

Don Agustín Velasco, the merchant, kept careful watch from inside the store with his sharp, beady eyes (eyes of a hawk, as his doting mother would say).

Even before Teodoro began making it a habit to station himself in front of the establishment, his appearance had attracted Don Agustín's attention. No *ladino* ever forgets the face of a *chamula* he has seen walking on the sidewalks (reserved for *caxlanes*), much less when he walks along slowly, like someone out for a stroll. It wasn't normal for this to happen, and Don Agustín wouldn't even have considered it to be possible. But now he had to admit that things could go even further: that an Indian could also have the audacity to stand in front of a showcase and look at what was displayed there, not only with all the aplomb of someone able to appreciate it, but with the somewhat insolent self-confidence of a buyer.

The narrow, yellow face of Don Agustín wrinkled into a disdainful grimace. For an Indian to buy candles for his saints, whiskey for his celebrations, or tools for his work on the Calle Real de Guadalupe is just fine. The people who deal with them there don't have illustrious names or bloodlines; they aren't heirs to fortunes, and it's their lot to do work of the lowest sort. One can put up with an Indian going into a pharmacy to ask for crushed elk's hoof, *aceite guapo*, or miraculous potions. Because when all is said and done, pharmacists only belong to families of mediocre rank, social-climbers who would like to exchange places with the best of them, so it's good that the Indians put them back in their place by frequenting their small businesses.

But for an Indian to turn to stone in front of a jewelry store... And not just any jewelry store, but the one belonging to Don Agustín Velasco, one of the descendants of the conquistadors, welcomed in the best of circles, esteemed by his colleagues, was—at the very least—inexplicable. Unless...

A suspicion began to gnaw away at him. What if this *chamula's* audacity rested on the strength of his tribe? It wouldn't be the first time, the merchant reflected bitterly. Rumors, where had he heard rumors about an uprising? Don Agustín quickly went over the places he had been during the last few days: the Bishop's palace, the Casino, Doña

Romelia Ochoa's social gathering.

How stupid! Don Agustín smiled at himself with condescending mockery. His Excellency the bishop, Don Manuel Oropeza, was so right when he declared that no sin goes unpunished. And Don Agustín, who had no taste for liquor or tobacco, who had rigorously abstained from carnal pleasures, was a slave to one vice: conversation.

He hovered around the town squares, the marketplace, even the Cathedral to trap people into conversation. Don Agustín was the first to dig up any gossip and to uncover scandal, and he lived to have others confide in him, to be the depository of secrets and to provoke intrigues. And at night, after his supper (a very rich hot chocolate that his mother rewarded him with for his daily toils and worries), Don Agustín would punctually attend some small gathering. There they gossiped, they told stories. About love-affairs, about squabbles over inheritances, about people who suddenly and inexplicably became wealthy, about duels. For several nights now the conversation had turned on a single theme: Indian uprisings. Everyone present had been a witness, a victim, a fighter or a victor in one or another. They recalled details about the main participants. Terrible scenes that made Don Agustín shudder with fear: fifteen thousand *chamulas* on the warpath, laying siege to Ciudad Real. The estates, sacked; the men, murdered; the women (no, no, one must drive away these bad thoughts), the women... to put it bluntly, raped.

Victory always came down on the side of the *caxlanes* (anything else would have been inconceivable), but at the cost of what enormous sacrifices, of what immense losses.

Do we learn from experience? Judging by that Indian standing in front of the showcase of his jewelry store, Don Agustín thought not. The inhabitants of Ciudad Real, caught up in their everyday tasks and concerns, had forgotten the past which should have served them as a lesson, and were living as if no danger threatened them. Don Agustín was horrified by such a lack of awareness. His own sense of security was so fragile that the face of a *chamula*, seen through a pane of glass, was enough to shatter it to pieces.

Don Agustín looked out toward the street again, with the unspoken hope that that Indian would no longer be there. But Méndez Acúbal still stayed on, immobile, attentive.

The passers-by walked past him with no sign of alarm or astonishment. This (and the tranquil sounds coming from the back of the house) restored Don Agustín's peace of mind. There was really no reason for him to be afraid now. The events at Cancuc, the siege of Pedro Díaz Cuscat at Jobel, the threats of Pajarito, couldn't happen again. These were different times, safer for decent people.

And besides, who was going to supply the arms, who was going to lead the rebels? This Indian here, with his nose flattened against the window of the jewelry store, was all alone. And if he was overstepping his bounds, no one was to blame but the *coletos* themselves. Why should anyone respect them, if they themselves didn't act like they should be respected? Don Agustín disapproved of the conduct of his fellow townsmen as if they had betrayed him.

"They say that some, very few by the grace of God, have stooped to the point where they will even shake an Indian's hand. The hand of Indians, a race of thieves!"

This judgement took on a particularly offensive taste in Don Agustín's mouth. Not only because of the sense of propriety that was as highly developed in him as it was in any member of his profession, but because of a particular circumstance.

Don Agustín wasn't honest enough to admit it, but he had a nagging suspicion that he was worthless. And what was even worse, his mother confirmed it in many ways. Her attitude toward this only child (a son of Saint Anne, she would say), born at a point when he was more of a bother than a consolation, was one of Christian resignation. The boy—his mother and the servants continued to call him that, even though Don Agustín was past forty— was very shy, easily frightened, and had absolutely no initiative. To think of all the good business opportunities he had let slip through his fingers! And all the ones he had thought were good, but that turned out to be nothing more than failures in the end! The Velascos' fortune had dwindled considerably since Don Agustín held the reins to their affairs. And as for the prestige of the firm, it was being maintained with difficulty, and only because of the respect everyone had felt towards the deceased man whom both mother and son still outwardly mourned.

But what else could you expect from a such a little mouse, from an "overgrown little boy"? Don Agustín's mother would shake her head and sigh. And she would redouble her flattery, her condescending words, her indulgences, because this was her way of being disdainful.

Instinctively, the merchant realized that he had before him a way to show everyone, even himself, how courageous he was. His zeal, his clear-sightedness, would be apparent to them all. And one simple word—thief—offered him the key: the man whose nose was flattened against the window of his jewelry store was a thief. There was no doubt about it. Besides, it was a very common occurrence. Don Agustín could think of all sorts of stories about burglaries and even large-scale robberies attributed to the Indians.

Satisfied with his reasoning, Don Agustín did not simply prepare to defend himself. His sense of solidarity with his race, his class and his profession demanded that he tell the other merchants about his fears, and together they went to the police. The neighborhood was put on the alert, thanks to Don Agustín's diligence.

But the cause for these precautions dropped out of sight for some time. Then, after several weeks, he showed up again in his usual place, and in the same stance: standing guard. Because Teodoro did not dare to go inside. No *chamula* had ever attempted to be that bold. If he were to take the risk and be the first, they would surely throw him out into the street before a single one of his lice could dirty the room. But even given the remote possibility that they didn't throw him out, if they allowed him to stay inside the store long enough to speak Teodoro wouldn't have known how to put his desires into words. He did not understand, he did not speak *Castilla*. In order to unstop his ears, and to loosen his tongue, he had been drinking *aceite guapo*. The liquor had infused him with a feeling of power. The blood coursed, hot and quick, through his veins. A sense of ease moved his muscles, dictated his actions. As though in a dream, he crossed the threshold of the jewelry store. But the cold and the dampness, the stench of stale, stagnant air, made him come back to his senses with a terrified start. From a jewelry case, the eye of a diamond gleamed out at him.

"What can I do for you, *chamulita*? What can I do for you?"

By repeating himself, Don Agustín was trying to gain time. Without looking, he felt for his pistol inside the top drawer behind the counter. The Indian's silence frightened him more than any threat. He didn't dare raise his eyes until he had the weapon in his hand.

His eyes met a gaze that paralyzed him. A gaze of surprise, of reproach. Why were they looking at him like that? It was not Don Agustín who was guilty. He was an honorable man, he had never hurt anybody. And now, he would be the first victim of these Indians who had suddenly appointed themselves judges! Here was the executioner, now, his foot ready to move forward, his fingers grasping inside the folds of his sash, ready to pull out who knows what instrument of death.

Don Agustín clenched the pistol tightly in his hand, but was incapable of firing it. He cried out to the gendarmes for help.

When Teodoro tried to run, he couldn't, because a mob had gathered at the doors of the store, cutting off his retreat. Shouts, menacing gestures, angry faces. The gendarmes shook the Indian, they questioned him, they searched him. When the silver coin appeared from within the folds of his sash, a triumphant cry excited the crowd. Don Agustín made vehement gestures as he held up the coin. The cries filled him with pride.

"Thief! Thief!"

Teodoro Méndez Acúbal was led off to jail. Since he was accused of such a common crime, none of the government bureaucrats was in a hurry to investigate it. His file turned yellow on the courthouse shelves.

Modesta Gómez

How cold the mornings are in Ciudad Real! A mist covers everything. From invisible places you hear the chimes of the first mass, the creak of massive doors opening, the wheeze of mills beginning to turn.

Huddled in the folds of her black shawl, Modesta Gómez was shivering as she walked back and forth. Her friend, Doña Agueda, the butcher, noticed:

"Some people don't have any stomach for this sort of work, they pretend they're too delicate, but what I think is that they're just plain lazy. The bad thing about being an ambusher is that you've got to get up so early."

I've always gotten up early, thought Modesta. That's how my mother raised me.

(No matter how she tried, Modesta couldn't remember her mother's scolding words, that face bending over her in early childhood. Too many years had gone by.)

They sent me away when I was just a little girl. One less mouth at home was a great relief for everyone.

Modesta could still remember the clean change of clothes they had dressed her in for the occasion. Then, suddenly, she found herself standing before an enormous door with a bronze knocker: a finely sculpted hand, with a ring entwined on one of its fingers. It was the house of the Ochoas: Don Humberto, owner of the "La Esperanza" store; Doña Romelia, his wife; Berta, Dolores and Clara, his daughters; and the youngest, his son Jorgito.

The house was full of marvelous surprises. What a feeling of wonder when Modesta discovered the drawing room! Cane furniture, wicker holders with fans of multicolored postcards spread out against the wall, the floor made of wood. Wood! A pleasant sensation of warmth rose from Modesta's bare feet all the way up to her heart. Yes, she was happy to stay with the Ochoas, to know that from now on this magnificent house would also be her home.

Doña Romelia led her to the kitchen. The servants gave the waddling little girl a hostile reception, and when they discovered that her hair was swarming with lice they unceremoniously dunked her into a vat filled with ice-cold water. They scrubbed her with soap-root, over and over again, until her braids were squeaky clean.

"All right, then. Now you look good enough to be presented to the *señores*. They're finicky enough already. But they really take a lot of pains with little Jorgito. Since he's the only boy..."

Modesta and Jorgito were almost the same age. And yet, she was the baby-carrier, the one who had to take care of him and keep him entertained.

"They say that my legs got twisted from carrying him around so much, because they weren't strong enough yet. Who knows?"

But the little boy was really spoiled rotten. If he couldn't have his own way, he went "completely nuts," as he himself used to say. They could hear him screaming all the way out to the store. Doña Romelia would hurry over.

"What did they do to you, lambkins, my little darling?"

Without breaking his wails even for a second, Jorgito would point to Modesta.

"The carrier?" the mother nodded. "We'll fix her so that she doesn't lay a finger on you again. Look, a smack here, right in the noodle, a yank on the ear and a whack on the behind. Is that better, my little dumpling, little apple of my eye? All right, you're going to have to let me go now; I have things to do."

In spite of these incidents, the children were inseparable. Together they suffered through all the childhood illnesses; together they discovered secrets; together they got into mischief.

Although this sort of intimacy relieved Doña Romelia from the extreme attention that her son demanded, it still struck her as uncalled-for. How could she ward off the risks? The only idea that occurred to Doña Romelia was to put Jorgito into primary school, and to forbid Modesta from using the familiar *vos* when she addressed him.

"He's your master, your *patrón*," she explained condescendingly, "and you can't be so chummy with the *patrones*."

While the boy was learning to read and count, Modesta was busy in the kitchen; feeding the fireplace, hauling in water, and gathering up slop for the hogs.

They waited until she was a little bigger, until she'd had her first period, to give Modesta a more important position. They put away the old mat she had slept on since first arriving, and replaced it with a cot that was going unused since a cook had died. Under the pillow Modesta placed her wooden comb and her mirror with its celluloid frame. By this time she was a robust little pole, and she liked to put on airs. When she went out to the street to run an errand, she washed her feet very carefully, scrubbing them with a stone. The starch in her skirts crackled as she walked past.

The street was the stage for her triumphs: young men, barefoot like her but with decent jobs and ready to marry, courted her with rough compliments; the "swells", Jorgito's friends, propositioned her; and wealthy old men offered her presents and money.

At night Modesta dreamed of being the lawfully married wife of an artisan. She could imagine the humble little house on the outskirts of Ciudad Real, having to scrape to make a living, the life of sacrifices that awaited her. No, better not. There would always be time enough for a legal marriage. Better to sew her oats first, to have a good time like bad women do. An old bawd would sell her, the kind that offers girls to gentlemen. Modesta could see herself in a corner of the brothel, wrapped in a shawl with her eyes lowered, while drunken, scandalous men made bids to see who would be the first to possess her. And then, if everything went well, the man who made her his mistress would set her up in a little business so she could support herself. Modesta would not hold her head up high, she wouldn't be a model of purity as though she had left the charge of her *patrones* heading for the church, all dressed in white. But maybe she would have a child with good blood, and a little savings. She would learn some trade. With time her reputation would grow, and they would call on her to grind chocolate or to cure evil spells in the homes of well-off people.

But instead, she had ended up being an ambusher. What a topsy-turvy world this is!

One night Modesta's dreams were interrupted. The door to the servants' room opened quietly, and in the darkness someone moved toward the girl's cot. Modesta felt heavy breathing close to her, and a rapidly beating pulse. She crossed herself, thinking it a ghost. But a hand fell brutally upon her body. She tried to scream, and her scream was smothered by another mouth covering her own. She and her adversary struggled while the other women slept soundly. From a scar on his shoulder, Modesta recognized Jorgito. She didn't try to defend herself any longer. She closed her eyes, and submitted to him.

Doña Romelia had suspicions about her son's hanky-panky, and the servants' gossip removed all doubt. But she decided to pretend that she knew nothing. After all, Jorgito was a man, not a saint; and he was at that age when the blood starts to boil. Besides, it was preferable for him to find release in his own home, instead of going around with tramps who teach boys bad habits and bring them to ruin.

Thanks to his rape of Modesta, Jorge could brag about being a "real" man. For several months he had been smoking in secret, and he had gone off and gotten drunk two or three times. But in spite of the taunts of his friends, he still hadn't dared to go with women. He was afraid of them: all painted up, so vulgar in their gestures and the way they talked. But with Modesta he felt comfortable. The only thing that worried him was that his family might find out what was going on between them. To mislead them, in front of everybody he treated Modesta coldly, and even with exaggerated harshness. But at night he again sought out that body he knew through long familiarity, in which the smells of home and childhood memories mingled together.

But as the saying goes, "What night hides is revealed by day." Modesta's complexion began to take on a mottled look; there were dark circles under her eyes and her movements were listless. The other servants made comments, accompanied by obscene winks and malicious laughter.

One morning Modesta had to stop her work grinding corn because a sudden attack of nausea swept over her. A tattletale went to notify the *patrona* that Modesta was pregnant.

Doña Romelia showed up in the kitchen like a fury.

"You ungrateful little slut. You would have to go off the deep end. And what did you think would happen? That I was going to cover up your carrying-on? Not on your life. I have a husband that I have to answer to, daughters that I need to have good examples for. So I want you out of here right now."

Before she left the Ochoas' house, Modesta was subjected to a humiliating search. The lady and her daughters went through the girl's clothing and possessions to make certain that she hadn't stolen anything. After that they formed a sort of barricade in the entryway, and Modesta had to go through it in order to leave.

Fleetingly, she glanced at those faces. Don Humberto's, ruddy from fat, with its watery little eyes; Doña Romelia's, twitching with indignation; the girls', Clara, Dolores and Berta's, curious and slightly pale with envy. Modesta looked for Jorgito's face, but he wasn't there.

Modesta had reached the town limits of Moxviquil. She stopped. Other women, barefoot and badly dressed just like her, were already there. They looked at her with distrust.

One of them spoke up for her: "Leave her alone. She's a Christian like anybody else, and she's got three kids to support."

"And what about us? Are we some kind of rich women?"

"Did we come here to sweep up money with a broom?"

"What this one takes isn't going to get us out of the poor-house. You've got to have a little pity. She was just left a widow."

"Who was her husband?"

"Alberto Gómez. The one who just died."

"The bricklayer?"

"The one who drank himself to death?"

(Although it was spoken in a low voice, Modesta could hear the remark. A violent flush spread across her cheeks. Alberto Gómez, the one who drank himself to death! Filthy lies! Her husband didn't die like that. All right, it was true that he did his share of drinking, even more than his share lately. But the poor man had good reason to. He was tired of wearing the pavement out looking for work. Nobody builds a house, nobody has repairs done when it's the rainy season. Alberto got tired of waiting on porticos or in doorways for the rains to stop. That's what got him going into bars in the first place. Bad company did the rest. Alberto neglected his obligations, he mistreated his family. You had to forgive him. When a man isn't in his right mind, he does one awful thing after another. The next day, when the haze wore off, it scared him to see Modesta all full of bruises, and the children in a corner, trembling with fear. He cried with shame and remorse. But he didn't change. Vice is stronger that reason.

While she waited up for her husband at all hours of the night, Modesta tortured herself thinking about the million things that could happen to him on the streets. A fight, a stray bullet, being run over. Modesta imagined him carried in on a stretcher, covered with blood, and she wrung her hands wondering where she was going to find money for the burial.

But things happened differently. She had to go get Alberto because he had fallen asleep on the sidewalk, and there the night found him and the evening dew fell on him. Alberto had no visible cuts or bruises. He complained a little about a pain in his side. They made him an ointment out of animal fat just in case he had taken a chill; they put cupping-glasses on him; he drank embered water. But the pain only got stronger. The death rattle was brief, and the neighbor women took up a collection to pay for the coffin.

"The cure turned out to be worse for you than the disease," Modesta's friend Agueda told her. "You married Alberto so you'd be under a man's hand, and so the son of the famous Jorge would grow up with some respect. And now you end up a widow, not a penny to your name, with three mouths to feed and nobody to look out for you."

It was true. And true also that the years Modesta was married to Alberto were years of pain and hard work. True that when he was drunk, the bricklayer beat her, throwing in her face how Jorgito had abused her, and true that his death was the biggest humiliation of all for her family. But Alberto had come through for Modesta at just the right time: when everyone had turned their backs on her so as not to see her dishonor. Alberto had given her his name and his legitimate children; he had made a lady out of her. How many of these beggars in widows' weeds talking behind her back wouldn't have sold their souls to the devil to be able to say the same thing!)

The early morning mist began to lift. Modesta had sat down on a rock. One of the ambushers approached her.

"*Yday*? Weren't you one of the clerks in Doña Agueda's butcher-shop?"

"I still am. But I don't make enough money there. With me and my three little ones I needed something extra. My friend Agueda told me about this."

"We only do it because when you're poor, you lead a dog's life. But being an ambusher wears you down. It's hardly worth it."

(Modesta searched the face of the woman talking to her, suspicious. What was the point of saying awful things like that? Probably to scare her off so she wouldn't be any competition. That was a big mistake. Modesta was no pansy: in other places she had gone through her own hard times. Because the business of being behind a butcher counter was no paradise either. Nothing but work all morning long: keeping the place clean—and with the flies there was never any end to it; taking care of the merchandise; bargaining with the clients. Those maids from rich houses who were always demanding the fattest pieces of meat, the best cuts, and the cheapest price! She had to give in to their wishes, but Modesta took out her revenge on the others. The ones who looked poor and badly dressed, the women who had stands in the market place and their employees, she held strictly to account; and if they ever tried to get their meat at another stand because it was a better deal, she would scream at them and never wait on them again.)

"Yes, handling meat is a dirty job. But it's even worse to be an ambusher. Here you have to fight with Indians."

(And where don't you have to? thought Modesta. Her friend Agueda had instructed her right from the start: for Indians you saved the spoiled or grainy meat, the big lead weight that tilted the scales, and your howls of indignation if he made even the slightest protest. The women who ran the other stands would come running over when they heard the outburst. A fight would break out, with gendarmes and people who were just curious joining in, egging on the participants with sharp words, insulting gestures and shoves. The outcome of the scuffle, invariably, was the Indian's hat or bag that the victor held up in the air like a trophy, and the vanquished's frightened run to escape the threats and mockery of the crowd.)

"Here they come now!"

The ambushers stopped talking in order to look toward the hills. Now they could make out some figures moving around in the mist. They were Indians, loaded down with the merchandise they were going to sell in Ciudad Real. The ambushers moved forward a few steps in their direction. Modesta imitated them.

The two groups were face to face. A few brief seconds of anticipation went by. Finally the Indians began walking again, their heads lowered, their eyes fixed obstinately on the ground, as if the magical recourse of not looking at the women would make them non-existent.

The ambushers threw themselves upon the Indians tumultuously. Stifling screams, they struggled with them for possession of objects they didn't want to damage. Finally, when the wool blanket or the net of vegetables or the clay utensil were in the ambusher's hands, she would take a few coins from her blouse, and without counting them, let them drop to the ground, where the fallen Indian would pick them up.

Taking advantage of the fight's confusion, a young Indian girl tried to escape, running away with her burden intact.

"That one's yours," one of the ambushers shouted jeeringly to Modesta.

Automatically, just like an animal trained for a long time in the hunt, Modesta threw herself after the fugitive. When she caught up to her she grabbed her skirt, and the two of them tumbled to the ground.

Modesta fought until she was on top of her. She pulled her braids, slapped her cheeks, dug her fingernails into her ears. Harder! Harder!

"You damn Indian! Now you're going to pay me for everything!"

The Indian girl writhed in pain. Ten thin lines of blood ran from her earlobes down to her neck.

"No more, Ma'am, no more..."

Inflamed, panting, Modesta held on to her victim. She didn't want to let go of her, not even when the Indian handed over the wool blanket she had been hiding. Another ambusher had to intervene.

"That's enough," she said forcefully to Modesta, pulling her to her feet.

Modesta staggered like a drunk while she used her shawl to wipe her face, dripping with sweat.

"And you," continued the ambusher, turning to the Indian, "quit sniveling: that's no way to act. Nothing's happened to you. Take this money and God help you. Be thankful we're not taking you to the Courthouse for causing a disturbance."

The Indian girl hastily picked up the coins, and quickly ran away. Modesta watched, uncomprehending.

"Let this be a lesson to you," the ambusher told her. "I'm keeping the blanket since I paid for it. Maybe tomorrow you'll have better luck."

Modesta nodded. Tomorrow. Yes, she would come back tomorrow, and the day after tomorrow, and forever. It was true what they said: an ambusher's job is hard, and there's not much profit in it. She looked at her bloody fingernails. She didn't know why. But she was satisfied.

Coming of the Eagle

In him, youth took on the profile of a bird of prey: eyes close together, a disappearing forehead, wide eyebrows. The stance of a man of daring: legs spread apart, feet firmly set, massive shoulders, hips that seemed to be made for wearing a gun. And above all, his name: Héctor Villafuerte.

But what can a man do with such a fever pounding in his head, in his blood, in his heart, when he lives in a town like Ciudad Real? And, as if that weren't enough, when he's the son of a widow?

His childhood home carries the odor of quince, of incense. Pots bubbling on the fire, small pots with ham-bone, timid pots of stew. Starched petticoats crackle at the touch of the wind, along the corridors, in the patios.

The altarboy's cassock just didn't suit Héctor's nature. Tucking it under his belt, he climbed trees, jumped over fences, got into savage fights with other wild little boys. After a week had gone by he had to return it, torn to shreds, to Father Domingo, who had cherished the hope of making a dynamic priest out of this rebellious boy, a missionary with real guts.

Héctor's school years were nothing but trouble. Cutting-up in class, bad grades, and finally a notorious expulsion "for being the leader of a riot that broke all the windows (not to mention smashing the doors, walls and furniture) in his classroom."

For him to learn a trade would have been a stain on the family honor. Safely preserved in a very old chest, they kept titles of nobility signed by the King of Spain himself, and a coat of arms, worn away by time, on the main facade of the house. Poverty is no disgrace to the man who has to endure it. But manual labor...

A sort of natural selection, that drew Héctor away from the sacristy, the classroom, and the workshops, had him wind up in the street with his friends, a cigarette dangling insolently from his lips, spitting in disdain. His friends led him to the filthy bed of a prostitute, to the worn table of a saloon, to the sordid atmosphere of the pool hall with its smoke and artificial light.

Héctor started hanging around with third-rate musicians. Wherever anyone was found playing the marimba, there he was too, helping to load or unload the instrument as carefully as though it were a cadaver. In time he became indispensable, with his boisterous shouts of "Viva!" to honor whoever was paying for the serenade. And at the break of dawn, he would fire someone's pistol in the air, expending in wasted gunpowder his rebellious spirit, that stallion which had been bridled — at such a young age — by routine.

He learned cheap tricks: how to cut a deck of cards and shuffle them, how to judge the quality of a fighting cock, and which is the best kind of hunting dog. To be a real gentleman, the only thing Héctor needed was money.

Because Héctor couldn't afford the luxury of being lazy. His mother began pawning jewelry to save him from the dishonor of a gambling debt. After that, it was easy to part with paintings, china, clothing. Buyers don't want trashy, old junk. They chisel you down; they're grumpy when they hand over money. And as a sort of vengeance, they treat you to a biting remark, a warning that barely conceals their inner smile of self-satisfaction, a piece of advice that's absolutely useless.

The widow fought to the very end to save the saints on the altar from her son's squandering. Then, when the altar was empty, the old woman lost the will to live. Her death was refined: no sudden jolt, not a hair out of place. Distant relatives, charitable ladies took up a collection to pay the funeral expenses.

During the first months after his mother's death, Héctor was obliged to put in an appearance at celebrations and festivities. He set himself apart, in keeping with the period of mourning, and from there he would watch the others eat and enjoy themselves. He viewed them distantly, because for him disdain was an essential attitude, not a temporary frame of mind.

When the knees of his pants began to take on a noticeable sheen, and when he had to step carefully so the soles wouldn't come off his shoes, Héctor decided the time had come to settle down.

He broadcast his intentions to the four winds, and made a great show of the fact that he was an eligible bachelor, convinced that his merchandise was the sort that was always in demand. The women looked at him hungrily, and Héctor reacted to all of them —making no distinctions so that he would not compromise himself— with the same smile of cynical expectation and indifferent sensuality.

If only Héctor at least had a horse to scar the cobblestones in the streets, to make sparks fly, proud and defiant! Be patient. You'll have that later. You will have a well-laid table, money in your wallet, respectful, servile greetings from the very people who avoid you or despise you now. The wife who will provide you a comfortable living and respect... well, any one of them would do. All women are the same in the dark. Héctor would fulfill his marital duties, getting her pregnant every year. What with her pregnancies and bringing up the children, she'll be satisfied, tucked away in her own little corner.

But as it happens, the women in Ciudad Real don't walk the city streets as free parties. If it were just up to them, they might, but there are fathers, brothers, walls and customs defending them. And it isn't simply a matter of pouncing on them, suddenly, like a wildcat. In the end, the elders always end up winning. Or cutting off an inheritance.

Héctor's attempts to marry came to nothing. The man wore the sidewalks smooth, whistling on street corners with the studied air of a big shot, attempting to flirt from time to time when he walked past a window. The girls fled from him, slamming the shutters closed. And once behind the window panes, they made fun of Héctor's advances, a little sad perhaps that they couldn't respond to him.

However, there was one woman with no relatives, no one looking out for her, only a respectable, elderly lady for the sake of appearances who took care of her house. But in everything else, she was free. She was already kind of gone to seed, a bit past her prime. She had a serious look, and a bitter purse to her lips. No man had ever approached her because, although she was believed to be wealthy, she had an even greater reputation for being a miser.

When a woman is in Emelina Tovar's condition, reasoned the suitor, she'll fall in love and let go of what she's holding on to. To make her fall in love would not be difficult. All he needed to do was wave a red flag in front of her, and she would charge in a blind fury, full of passion.

Against all of Héctor's predictions, Emelina did not charge. She watched the gallant walking around under her balcony, and she knit her brows even tighter in a supreme effort of alertness. That was all. Not one flutter of impatience, not one sigh of hope in that dried-up old maid's breast.

When Héctor finally managed to speak to her for the first time, Emelina listened to him, blinking as though a harsh light were bothering her. She didn't know how to reply. And in this silence the suitor understood he had been accepted.

The wedding was hardly what you would call dazzling. The groom was handsome, that's true, but he didn't have a red cent to his name. And on top of that, he was a spendthrift.

Emelina walked down the aisle of the La Merced church (because she had made a vow to the Virgin, so miraculous, to be married at her altar) holding on tightly to Héctor's arm, somewhat awed, still overcome by this precarious triumph that destiny had favored her with at the end of a long, humiliating loneliness.

Emelina supported herself by making sweets. Insects were always buzzing around the inner patio of her house where the *chimbos*, *acitrones*, and *tartaritas* lay drying in the sun. The business didn't bring in much. But a methodical, frugal woman can save. Not enough to amass a fortune, but certainly enough to face any unexpected situation, an illness, some sort of difficulty. How many of those this husband was going to bring her, this man who was younger, wild, and looking out only for himself!

If Emelina had not been in love with Héctor, she might have been happy. But her love was a wound that always lay open, that the other person's slightest frown and most insignificant action could cause to bleed. She was racked with jealousy and desperation in the bed he so frequently abandoned. A bird of Héctor's category isn't satisfied with mere canary seed. He breaks out of his cage and flies away.

Meanwhile, the newlywed husband still couldn't figure it out. What about his wife's money? He went through trunks, he looked under mattresses, he dug holes all over. Nothing. That clever woman had hidden it well, if she had it to start with.

The fact is that the savings were gone after the first few months, and they had to dip into capital. It all went for Héctor's carousing, his binges, his gambling losses.

Then, suddenly, it ended. Emelina could not survive a difficult childbirth that her age made impossible. And Héctor was left alone, miraculously free again. And out in the street.

What are friends for? They're for difficult times, just like this one. The man who was your drinking buddy yesterday has a responsible position today, and he can recommend you to someone just by saying a word.

"Do you know how to write, Héctor? A little. All right. Bad handwriting, terrible in spelling. If only you'd learned when your mother, God rest her soul, was paying for your schooling! But this is no time for blaming anyone. Read without any stumbling, yes. And math? So-so, that's all. I can't promise you anything. But, anyway, we'll see what we can do."

A few months later Héctor Villafuerte was appointed Municipal Secretary of the town of Tenejapa.

Unfortunate town! The Town Hall, the parish church, and a few houses of the *ladinos* are made of adobe. Everything else is huts made of sticks. Muddy streets, weeds, open fields around the first corner. There's trash everywhere, and farm animals and naked children wandering all over the place.

"What a mess you're in now!" Héctor said to himself. Without a soul you can talk to, all alone, since the *ladinos* around here are absolute nobodies, and Indians aren't people at all. They don't understand Christian language. They bow their heads and say, yes sir, yes ma'am, yes *ajwalil.* They don't even raise their heads when they get bombed. One drink after another, and not one shout for joy, not even a snort of pleasure. They just turn as still as stones, and all of a sudden fall flat on their faces. I wouldn't even want to rub shoulders with one of them. There's an old saying: If you walk with wolves, you'll end up howling. And I don't have a prayer of getting out of this rat-hole. What filthy little salary I make goes just for me to live and get my clothes cleaned. There's no way even to get some extra bucks. It looks like the only lake you can jump into around here is to sell raw whiskey. At festivals or on market days all the *ladinos* set up stands in their entryways. The Indians go inside very proper, and they come out falling-down drunk. You can't even walk on the streets with all the bodies lying around. Maybe I'd be better off if I was a hirer. But where would I get the money to set myself up?

Municipal Secretary! A lovely title! A person would almost think that Héctor held a position of real importance. But he handled only the most trivial cases: stolen chickens, sheep, or at worst, cows. Crimes having to do with witchcraft or jealousy, fights between drunks. Personal acts of revenge in which nobody felt they had any right to get involved. But you better believe it, every case demanded an official report for each and every detail.

"What a stingy business this Government is!" lamented Héctor.

"They expect you to live off of thin air. The dignity of a man's appointment doesn't mean a thing. A Municipal Secretary is someone these ignorant people should respect. And who's going to take me seriously if I go around like a beggar? One tiny, little room to work in, to eat in, and to sleep in. And you really have to take your hat off to the furniture! A cot made out of rope, and a table and chairs that give you the creeps just looking at them. Even the official seal is so old that it won't stamp anymore. And these miserable people want every piece of paper to carry their big seal. What a bunch of crap!"

After he'd had this conversation with himself, Héctor refused to compose documents any longer. We don't have a seal, he told the Indians sourly. And without a seal, no matter what I write, it's going to be worthless.

Silently, the delegation of "leaders" left. They stayed out in the corridor of the Municipal Palace for a while, whispering together. Then they went back into Héctor's room. The eldest of the men spoke for them all.

"We would like to know, *ajwalil*, what you meant when you said that the seal was worn out."

"What is the seal?" another old man asked humbly.

"It's the eagle," the functionary replied in an arrogant tone.

The Indians understood. At one time or another they had all seen its image on the national emblem. And they had imagined that the mission of its wings was to carry complaints and allegations to the feet of justice. And so it was that the town of Tenejapa would drown in unresolved criminal accusations, in documents incapable of taking flight.

"How did the eagle wear out?"

They all posed the question with the same sense of amazement that people have in times of great natural disasters. Héctor Villafuerte shrugged to avoid giving an answer that these stupid Indians wouldn't have understood anyway.

"But then, can't you get another eagle?" one of them asked cautiously.

"Who's going to pay for it?" interrupted Héctor.

"That depends, *ajwalil*."

"How much does one cost?"

Héctor stroked his chin to help him calculate. He wanted to make himself appear important to them with the price of the tools he used. Then he stated:

"A thousand pesos."

The Indians looked at each other in fright. As though the figure carried some power that turned them all mute, a great silence filled the room. Héctor's burst of laughter broke it:

"So! That got you, didn't it? A thousand pesos!"

"Isn't there an eagle that's any cheaper?"

"What do you think, you damn Indian? That you can bargain for one the way you do when you buy a yard of cloth or a drink? The eagle isn't just some little trinket; it's the *nahual* of the Government."

What an absurd conversation! If he kept it going, it was only because Héctor was bored, because he wanted to keep up the facade of his infallible judgement.

"All right, *ajwalil.*"

"Until tomorrow, then, *ajwalil.*"

"Good night, *ajwalil.*"

The Indians left. But the next day, first thing in the morning, there they were again.

"We want to file a petition, *ajwalil.*"

"Don't you understand anything? A petition is worthless unless it has the seal of the eagle on it."

"Doesn't the paper talk?"

"No, it doesn't talk."

"All right then, *ajwalil.*"

"Good-bye, *ajwalil.*"

The Indians left again. But they didn't go far from the City Hall; they walked around outside, arguing about the problem.

"Now what are they up to?" Héctor wondered nervously. He had heard stories about *ladinos* whose houses had been burned down, who had been chased over the hills by Indians with machetes.

But the "leaders'" intentions seemed to be peaceful. As the afternoon arrived, they went their separate ways.

The next day the group was there again, clearing their throats, not daring to speak. Finally, one of them went over to Héctor.

"How was the little bird when it woke up this morning, *ajwalil*?"

"What little bird?" retorted Villafuerte, in a bad mood.

"The one on the paper."

"Oh, the eagle. I already told you: it died."

"But you must have another one."

"No, I don't."

"Then, where can you get one?"

"In Ciudad Real."

"When are you going there?"

"When me and my balls are good and ready. Besides, where's the cash coming from?"

"How much do you need?"

The Indians' persistence was going beyond mere stubbornness. There was real interest there. Suddenly Héctor realized that the opportunity he had been dreaming about for so long was here, just waiting for him to grab it. In a casual tone of voice, even though he could barely contain the excitement this realization produced in him, he said flatly:

"I'll need five thousand pesos."

"You said one thousand the first time."

"That's a lie! Who knows more about this, you or me? It says right here (Héctor feverishly opened the first book his eyes fell on and held it up to the Indian): the eagle costs five thousand pesos."

The Indians' determination collapsed. Without another word they all went outside to deliberate. Villafuerte watched them leave, worried.

"I was too greedy for my own good. I went too far asking for so much money. Where are those poor fools going to get it? But then, what do I care? Let them work for it, hire themselves out to the plantations on the coast, borrow it, dig up their money-jars. I'm not going to go feeling sorry for them. What a joke! As if I didn't know that they don't give a second thought to shelling out tons of pesos for a *brujo* or to celebrate their saints' days. When it comes to the Church, they're generous enough, all right: a mass with three priests, a big jubilee. Why should the Government be treated any different?"

Héctor finally convinced himself that buying the seal was an absolute necessity, and that he had offered a reasonable price. He hardened in his decision not to compromise.

But Indians are stubborn. They come and they go, always hammering away at the same tune.

"Make it two thousand pesos, *ajwalil*. That's all we can raise."

"What's the eagle for, anyway? You think I want it for myself?"

"You know how poor we are, *patrón*."

"Don't come crying to me, you scum."

"How about three thousand pesos, sir."

"I said five thousand."

They kept trying to bargain, carried along by simple inertia. The Indians knew that in the end, they would have to give in.

That night, by the light of an oil-lamp, Héctor counted his treasure one more time. Old coins, saved for God knows how many centuries. Images out of time, inscriptions that could no longer be deciphered. Their owner had been so tight-fisted that he wouldn't hand them over to anybody: not when he was sunk in the depths of misery, not even spurred on by hunger. And now they would be used to buy the picture of a bird.

Héctor went off to Ciudad Real, followed by the escort of "leaders." When he grew tired of riding his horse, his *tayacanes* had the litter ready. Héctor traveled over the most dangerous stretches of the road on the backs of Indians.

The Indians submitted to this demand humbly. By doing this, they became worthy of carrying the seal on their return.

Because, as Villafuerte instructed them, the seal is a highly prized object. To guard against thieves stealing it, they had to hide what they were doing. If they pretended that the trip had another purpose, like business for example, then no one would bother them.

And so in Ciudad Real Héctor bought great quantities of merchandise: food, candles, and above all, liquor. In one of the many packages that the Indians carried lay the famous seal.

Back in Tenejapa, Héctor Villafuerte found a place to open his store. Those five thousand pesos (four thousand nine hundred ninety, to be exact, because the seal cost him ten) were the basis of his fortune. Héctor prospered. He was able to marry again, and this time to his own liking. The girl was young, submissive, and as a dowry she brought a herd of cattle.

But Héctor didn't want to give up his position as Municipal Secretary. In his dealings with the other merchants, it brought him prestige, influence, authority.

And besides, seals don't last forever. The one he was using now was already wearing out. Already the lines of the eagle were almost unrecognizable. Already it only looked like a smudge of ink.

The Fourth Vigil

Little Nides awoke at midnight, her coarse cotton night shirt soaked with sweat. For heaven's sake, it had almost happened this time! The Carranzistas were coming, those Carranclanes who act like mule-drivers and don't show any respect for anything. They slammed the iron clapper — bam-bam — against the large, wooden door. Little Nides ran all through the house like a crazy woman, looking for a hiding place for the trunk...

Fortunately, just at the very moment the Carranzistas were about to break down the door, she woke up. With her knotted fingers, all twisted up from rheumatism, Little Nides groped in the dark until she found the matches. She lit the tallow candle. A flickering, yellowish light spread across the room. The old woman's silhouette was cast grotesquely onto the bare walls. In one of the corners you could still see the faded spot where the trunk had been.

For a few seconds Little Nides stared at the spot. It took that long until concrete reality swept aside the terror of her dream: the trunk was safe, and it wouldn't matter if the Carranzistas came.

How she had debated before putting the trunk away in a safe place! Little Nides had pored over one book after another, thinking of how she would be able to manage it. Finally, one afternoon she stepped out the front door. A few children were playing *chepe-loco* up and down the street, but they were so busy with their game that they wouldn't notice anything. In the distance Little Nides could see a *chamula* coming all alone, as though he had been sent to carry out her plan. Little Nides quickly motioned to him, then hid behind the door to wait.

The Indian came in, his pants rolled up nearly to his knees, a machete wrapped in his poncho.

"How much are you going to pay?" he asked, even before he knew what the work was.

Little Nides answered with the first figure that came into her mind: twenty *reales*. The *chamula* scratched his head, uncertain if it was a great deal or very little. But he accepted.

Together, they walked to a place that Little Miss Nides pointed out to the Indian, a spot she had chosen carefully so that the roots of the fruit trees would not be damaged.

"Put your machete over there, fellow. You won't need it," Missy Nides told the man, handing him a spade.

Before he took it, the Indian asked again about his pay. What a stubborn dolt!

"I already told you: twenty *reales*."

"Yes, that's what you said all right. But at the last minute, when I finish my work, you'll start yelling that I'm a thief and they'll come and throw me out of the house."

Little Nides told him no, to stop being so brutish and to hurry up because soon it would be dark.

The man began to dig. A large hole, because Little Nides remembered her grandmother's advice very well: the trunk ought to fit inside easily, and there should still be room left over for a body. In a situation like this, it doesn't do any good to cut out the tongue of whoever helps you. They'll just come back and point, and then other people will dig up what you've buried.

Little Nides sat down at the base of a tree to watch the Indian work. Large shovelfuls of earth were coming out, one after another, and dirt was piling up next to the hole. If he keeps on like this, he'll be finished in no time, thought the woman. That's good! Yes, now let the Carranzistas come whenever they want to.

Moving the trunk was no problem. The Indian lifted it up with one hand, and when he was bending over to lay it in the bottom of the hole, Little Nides came up from behind and hit him with the flat side of the spade. The man didn't even grunt. His body fell heavily to the bottom.

Little Nides threw his poncho in on top, and she began to cover him with dirt, using the very same spade. What a lot of work! She wasn't used to all this moving around: her fingers got stiff, and a cramp gripped her shoulder. When she had finished, she was sweating, the same way she was now as she woke up from the nightmare.

Little Nides picked up the machete that the Indian had left leaning against the wall. It was well made and not very old, so she put it away in the storage room, along with the spade.

With a great effort, because at her age she was in no condition for this romping around, Little Nides went back to the burial place to tamp down the ground and to plant a hibiscus bush as a marker.

Trembling with cold now that the sweat had dried, Little Nides looked once more, uneasily, at the faded spot where the trunk had been. To get rid of it she would have had to wash the entire floor with a good deal of soap and a stiff brush. At her age, with all her aches and pains, she had no appetite for that.

"And if I get someone else to do it for me, they're just going to sit and stew, trying to guess where I hid the trunk."

Little Nides got to her feet with some difficulty, and attempted to drag the bed over on top of the spot. But the bed was too heavy (it was the one her grandmother had slept in), and there was no other furniture in the room.

Little Nides sat down, discouraged. Until now she had never noticed the fact that she had so little furniture. Her grandmother, a huge woman with a goiter that made her voice sound hoarse like it was coming up from the bottom of a kettle, hadn't lived in a place any better than this. And she dressed so badly that one time a stranger on the street, taking pity on her misery, gave her some money as an act of charity. Doña Siomara accepted it with a sly little laugh of gratitude. She, who owned so many properties up in the high country, and some of the best houses in Ciudad Real! But she didn't like to put on airs and she saved wherever she could. When workers hired by the week came in from her ranches, her orders were that not even the usual daily pot of stew be put on the fire, but for everyone to eat the *tostadas* and *posol* that the Indians brought as part of their own provisions.

"The hen fills her belly one grain at a time," Doña Siomara always used to say. "Where are the people who stuff themselves, who throw away their capital on luxuries and fancy feasts? They're running all sorts of risks, heading down the road to problems and debts, driving themselves to ruin."

Doña Siomara, on the other hand, had her trunks filled with hundred of gold pieces, and with heavy silver coins from Guatemala. She wouldn't let anyone even get close to them. No one, except her favorite granddaughter, Leonides Durán.

Because Little Nides, as her grandmother called her from the time she was born, was different from all the others. She wasn't mischievous as a baby, or wild as a girl. She didn't spend the whole day peeking out from the balcony, and she didn't stuff fistfuls of cotton into her bodice like her cousins, to go to dances. She never tried to cover up her defects.

"If someone comes courting you," her grandmother told her, "let him know what he's getting, don't let him feel later on that he was fooled. Besides, you can hold your head high, no matter where you are. Because one of these trunks —the biggest one— is going to be yours."

Little Nides looked at the trunk, her trunk, and then she didn't care if they didn't come around to serenade her, or if they didn't say pretty things to her at the bazaars, or if they didn't send her camellias wrapped in rice-paper when she went for a stroll through the park. She had other things to keep her entertained. When she and her grandmother were left all alone in the huge house, they opened the trunks up to count the money. What a special noise the paper rolls made when they tore open and the coins spilled out into her lap! How heavy they felt there! And what a pungent, penetrating odor they had!

If it was a nice day, Doña Siomara and Little Nides would go out to the patio, and after locking all the doors tight, would make a blanket of money laid out on straw mats. The two of them would look at the glints of gold and silver, and smile in silence.

So it was that time passed, and one by one Little Nides' cousins got married: Maria to a shopkeeper, Hortensia to a pharmacist, Lupe to a hirer. They could have found better matches if they'd been a little more patient. Doña Siomara wasn't going to live forever. But the girls never understood what was best for them, and they made their own bed... Then the children came along.

Every night the three girls came, along with their husbands, to visit Doña Siomara, and they talked about whatever happened to be going on, and they complained about their troubles. But deep down inside the only thing they were thinking about was the trunks.

Suddenly, no one knew how, rumors started to fly: that revolution had broken out in Mexico, that Pancho Villa's men were coming, that Carranza's men were coming. The streets of Ciudad Real were filled with dead bodies from one faction or the other. And anyone with two ounces of sense and a dollar in their pocket thought it best to leave for Guatemala.

All but Doña Siomara, who stuck to her guns, saying keep the shop, and the shop will keep thee, saying care clings to wealth. Why take a chance? She refused to go. She buried all the trunks in the inner patio of the house, and in the very last hole she also buried a *chamula*.

But was there any secret that could remain hidden in all that turmoil? Whatever wasn't known was invented. And before the idea even entered Doña Siomara's head, people had already accepted it as fact, and were spreading it around on every corner: she had buried her money.

And of course, when the Carranzistas arrive, what's the first thing they do? Well, they arrest Doña Siomara for "concealment of assets", and they threaten to kill her unless she reveals where she hid her treasure.

They said the old lady just sat withering away in jail, that even her wattles looked all dried up, like a turkey's. But it wasn't from hunger or fear; instead it was a sort of obstinacy. She was determined not to talk.

But while she was resisting, they came and searched her house. They lifted up slabs in the floors, knocked holes in the walls, tore down cupboards. Until they discovered the hiding place in the inner patio.

When Doña Siomara came out of jail she found her trunks nice and clean on the outside, without a speck of dust on them, and stuffed with the worthless scrip that the Carranzistas had put there in place of the money.

Who could survive such a terrible sense of rage? Doña Siomara died, delirious, with Little Nides never leaving the side of her bed. To her she dictated her dying wish: that one of the trunks be given to each of the granddaughters. And that she herself keep the largest one, just as she had always been promised.

No one attended the wake. Who would have something kind to remember about the dead woman, or an obligation to fulfill, or a favor to be grateful for, or a gift to expect? And Hortensia, Maria and Lupe's husbands were getting drunk in the saloons and shouting their anger to the four winds about an inheritance that had vanished into thin air.

So Little Nides, with only her thoughts for company, wrapped the dead woman in a shroud, took her to the mausoleum, and divided up the trunks as she had been instructed.

Meanwhile something was going on in the Government, since no one could buy anything because there was nothing to buy, or sell anything because no one had money, and food prices were sky-high. The fact of the matter was that when the storm was over, nothing was left where it had been before. Doña Siomara's houses were now in the possession of riffraff, and all the herds of cattle had disappeared from the ranches, and finally, the agrarian interests came to drop the final curtain over the rest of it.

Little Nides took her trunk and went to live in a tiny little room that didn't even have a toilet, and every now and then she had to put up with the shame of asking one of the neighbor ladies to allow her to use the little girls' room.

How was she going to support herself? Her grandmother hadn't prepared her for any job except counting gold and silver coins, and taking them out to shine in the sun. And she was no longer at an age where she could learn a trade.

But the truth is that while God tightens the noose, He doesn't strangle, and Little Nides had the gift of reading clearly. So, although she had never been very devout, they hired her to recite the novenas. People liked the timber of her voice, and the way she emphasized the most insignificant words and made mysterious pauses that seemed heavy with omens and promises.

Very early in the morning Little Nides would go to the Cathedral, and kneeling before the altar of the saint of the person who had paid for the prayers, slowly and carefully she would carry them out.

Years later her cousins began to come into their own. Thanks be to God, their husbands' businesses had nothing to do with ranches. And with her savings, Hortensia bought a place with fruit trees on the edge of town. What would it cost her to make a little wood-shingle house for Little Nides? And besides, she could keep watch to make sure that dirty, little Indians didn't come and steal the peaches and the red and green apples.

Little Nides found every excuse not to move. The place was too far away, and with her rheumatism it would be hard for her to get to town to do her jobs. Besides, if a robber came (Little Nides said robber, but she was thinking about the Carranzistas), who would protect her trunk?

"That's a good one!" Hortensia replied. "A trunk full of worthless scrip. We burned ours years ago."

Little Nides frowned. Burn her trunk! That would be the last thing she'd do, and only if she went mad. But she didn't like to argue, and when they mentioned the advantage of not having to pay rent, she made up her mind. Besides, ever since the Government had closed the churches, that business of the novenas hardly gave her enough to make ends meet.

Little Nides lived better at the orchard. When the young boys and the servant girls came to pick the fruit, she watched to make certain that they filled the baskets. If she had been anyone else, she would have set aside her own little supply of ripe peaches. But Little Nides never thought for a moment about taking advantage of anything. She had enough to eat at the houses of her friends.

She ate at other people's tables without any real eagerness, without humility, and perhaps even without gratitude. She was in no hurry to do little favors, because that was something servants did; she didn't get involved in spreading malicious gossip or in listening to shameful secrets. Why should I debase myself if I have my trunk? she told herself. I'm just as good as anybody else. Everyone respected her, and her silent presence had become so customary that whenever she wasn't there, the ladies of the house sent someone to inquire after her health, or they sent her a snack just so she could have a taste, and invited her to come as soon as she could.

Little Nides kept herself alive with those snacks when the wet weather made her rheumatism act up, and she stayed inside to rub on liniments.

She was happy because she still hadn't touched the money in her trunk, not even in the worst of times when she had that serious illness and the doctors had even met together to discuss her case. There she had really been clever, because she acted like she was dying, and everyone said it was a real shame but the only thing to do was pay her expenses. It made them feel bad that a granddaughter of Doña Siomara Durán should end up in the County Hospital like a common beggar.

But, they whispered at her bedside, what was the point of the sort of life Little Nides led? And yet, the sick woman wanted to live, she held onto life with the single-minded tenacity of those who don't waste their energy on frills, but never stop going.

Despite the doctors' predictions and the quick pessimism of her relatives, Little Nides lived. How could she die and abandon her trunk?

Now, though, she felt at peace. At the bottom of a hole, under the body of a *chamula* with a broken neck, rested her treasure.

"They say that where there is a body, a spirit appears," said Little Nides, and she could feel a shiver of terror about to run up her spine. Involuntarily, she looked outside, and through the window and the darkness, tried to make out the hibiscus bush.

A hoarse laugh, that kind of convulsive laugh that in old people quickly becomes a cough, shook her for a moment.

"But how could a spirit possibly appear if the body belonged to an Indian, and not to a rational person ?"

Feeling better, Little Nides snuffed out her candle and went to bed. She was going to sleep a little longer. It was a while yet before daybreak.

The Wheel of Hunger

"but give me at least,
in Spanish,
something to drink, to eat, to live on, a place to rest,
and then I will leave."
—César Vallejo

Alicia Mendoza awoke with a pain in her neck and her back. What a long trip! Hour after hour on this bus. Then the delay when they had to stop and change a tire. During the entire trip the motor had cranked over with difficulty.

There was nothing especially attractive about the scenery. Arid land, desert plants. It was already dark by the time they passed through Oaxaca. Alicia looked out the window, since she wanted to write and tell her friend Carmela that she had seen this city, the most important one along the route. But the only thing she could make out was the bustle and noise of the station.

The rest of the night, Alicia tried to sleep. The seat was uncomfortable, and a lady who was much too fat took up part of her space. But she did everything she could to make herself as comfortable as possible and to stay asleep until daybreak.

"It's so cold!" she muttered, as she breathed into her cupped hands. The bus moved along through a dense fog. Breaking through the mist, one could catch a fleeting glimpse of the crests of hills or the branches of pine trees passing by.

Alicia was about to close her eyes again when the lady sitting next to her warned:

"You'd better get ready. We're almost there."

She smiled, all bundled up in her woolen shawl. She seemed anxious to start a conversation. But Alicia wasn't paying attention to her. Was that town Ciudad Real, with its houses beginning to appear here and there along the road? She hadn't imagined it like this. When they told her she would be going to Chiapas, she had immediately pictured a jungle: bungalows with ceiling fans like in the movies, large glasses of iced drinks. Not this cold, this fog, these cottages with wood-shingle roofs... What a shame! The clothes she had bought for herself wouldn't do at all.

With my first paycheck I'm going to have to buy a coat, she thought, savoring the words proudly: "my first paycheck." Alicia's godmother had died feeling worried that she hadn't been able to get her trained for some job or for a profession.

"What are you going to do when I'm gone?" she wept. "If I could at least have seen you settled..."

As if it were that easy! She had no vocation whatsoever for becoming a nun, and as for getting married, the fiance was missing.

"Short, but badly stacked." That's the way a guy on the street once described Alicia. Boys didn't find her attractive, but they knew she was kind-hearted, and they treated her with brotherly affection. Little by little she became a confidante to all the young men in her crowd. She kept their secrets, she delivered love notes for them, she gave them advice about their problems, and quietly she waited her turn, in that constant shuffle of boyfriends and girlfriends taking place around her.

Her godmother let her stay with her. Poor Alicia! An orphan, with a stepmother who hated her from the start, who never wanted to have to take care of her.

"For me, on the other hand, a widow with no children, Alicia has been a comfort. So obedient, so kind. She really would make a good wife. But men these days only pay attention to a figure and a pretty face."

To make up for it somehow, her godmother bought her clothes and costume jewelry. She spent all her savings on that sort of thing. Until her illness started.

The diagnosis was clear and final: terminal cancer. But Alicia believed in miracles, and right up to the end she had faith that her godmother would get well. Santa Rita de Casia, advocate for impossibilities, was there anything she couldn't do? If I ask her for help, she'll be cured, Alicia thought. And all the while, she continued to take care of her godmother in self-abnegation. During those months of suffering, Alicia learned to give injections, to look at wounds without feeling repugnance, to change dressings, to distinguish between the countless medicine bottles, and to know which ones to use at the proper time.

Every cloud has a silver lining. It was that training that made it possible for Alicia to find work as a nurse later on.

It all happened in a way that Alicia liked to call Providential. Her friend Carmela, who had been with her during her mourning and who was concerned about her future (besides the fact that she had good social contacts), told her about a position in the Indian Aid Mission, in Chiapas.

"Is it connected with the Church?" exclaimed Alicia, her feelings too confused to let her analyze the matter.

"Don't be an idiot!" shot back Carmela. "You know how poor the church is. And at times like these when there's so much heresy!"

Alicia sighed as though a weight had been lifted from her shoulders. She had always been afraid she would end up in the iciness of Alaska in a nun's habit.

"Then it's funded by the government," Alicia deduced apprehensively.

"No, it's not that either. It's a private organization. It gets its support from charity, from people of means. The ones they call the administrators of God's wealth on earth."

"Oh, yes. Those high society ladies who put on charity teas and fashion shows."

Carmela gave her an acid look.

"Not them exactly, but their husbands. Businessmen, the kind who belong to clubs where they get together for banquets once a month. Distinguished people. You probably don't even know their names."

"Then they must be very demanding. And I don't have a degree."

"That's no problem. I know some people who can help us... Besides, you have experience, and that's what's important. And don't worry. The mission is just barely starting up. They don't pay much, but you'll have to accept what they offer, okay? And besides that they send you to the ends of the earth. They can't allow themselves the luxury of being too demanding."

"All right. Do you know where they would send me?"

"To a clinic in Chiapas. Well, a sort of clinic. Besides, it's the only one. The mission has run into a lot of problems. I understand that the house is very small. And there's only one doctor."

"His wife and I will keep each other company."

"I'm not sure that he's married," answered Carmela.

That uncertainty cleared away all the objections Alicia was going to make to the offer of a job. "Chiapas is so very far away, and I won't have anyone to look after me; the salary is only a drop in the bucket..." It doesn't matter, she kept telling herself impatiently. There are other advantages. If she had been asked, she wouldn't have been able to say what they were. But, in fact, she began to fantasize about living a great adventure in the jungle with a professional man, an elegant bachelor in love with her. There was only one way it could end, and that was in marriage. And Alicia, now the doctor's wife, would be happy, putting up little linen curtains on the clinic's windows, and raising their children (a lot of them, as many as God granted) in the healthy country air.

Alicia lavishly spent all the money her godmother had left her, buying herself clothes (low-cut dresses, because of the heat, but decent), and she bought a bus ticket. Carmela went to see her off at the station.

"Is this your first visit to Ciudad Real?" asked the woman sitting next to her.

"Yes."

"You have family or business interests around here, I suppose?"

"No. I'm coming here to work."

"For the Government?"

There was already a certain note of suspicion in her voice.

"At the Indian Aid Mission."

"Ah."

The monosyllable was spoken in a sarcastic tone that Alicia didn't understand. She wanted to continue the conversation, but the other lady seemed very preoccupied with counting her bags and got off the bus without saying goodbye.

The fog had lifted by now, but the day was unpleasant and gray. The women walked along the sidewalk, bundled up in thick black shawls.

"Carry your bag, Miss?"

This was a boy talking to Alicia, about ten years old, barefoot, with long, straggly hair. Several others gathered around him to try to beat him out of the job. He got rid of them by hitting and threatening them. The winner at last, he repeated his question. Alicia hesitated for a moment, but there was nothing to do but accept.

"Is there a hotel here that's decent and not too expensive?"

The boy nodded, and the two of them set off walking. The plaza, the porticos. The cathedral clock chimed eight times. Alicia had to move aside constantly to avoid bumping into Indians who, burdened down with their loads, walked quickly, anxiously. Others sat placidly on the sidewalk, picking off lice or going through their nets of food. As they passed near to one of them, the boy reached out and hit him sharply on the head. Alicia suppressed a cry of alarm: she was afraid this would lead to some drawn-out, troublesome incident. But the Indian didn't even turn around to see who had hit him, and Alicia and the boy continued on their way.

"Why did you hit him?" she finally asked.

The boy scratched his head, perplexed.

"Well... just because."

In Alicia's heart a battle took place between her natural timidity and her sense of ethics. She finally decided to counsel the boy, and she tried to keep any harshness, any note of acrimony, out of her words as she cautioned him never to do that again, for next time he might not get off so easily.

"One of them could stand up to you... and they are older men, much stronger than you..."

The boy smiled mockingly.

"What do you think I am? Some sort of an Indian down at their level?"

They had come to the hotel. It had a dismal appearance. A big, ramshackle house with numbers painted crudely on the doors to its rooms.

A fat, placid woman came out to meet them. Alicia told her that she would be staying only a short time: just long enough to rest and freshen up a little. If she showed up looking like this, she said, pointing to her wrinkled clothing and her mussed hair, her superiors would get a bad impression of her.

"I came to work at the Indian Aid Mission," she finished, watching to see what effect these words would have on the other woman.

The woman showed no sign of disapproval. But when it came time to pay the bill, the final amount had been changed.

"You people (she told Alicia in answer to her protests) come to Ciudad Real to make life more expensive for us. When the Indians start rebelling, they won't work on the ranches without pay any more, they won't sell their goods at the prices they charged before. We're the ones who suffer. It's only right that you people should pay for the damage you do to us."

Alicia didn't understand her reasoning, but the landlady's authoritarian tone intimidated her. Hours later she told the Mission director about the incident. He was a middle-aged man with no title but, rumor had it, with excellent administrative abilities.

"Well, now you're getting your initiation, Alicia. As soon as they find out that you work with us, the shopkeepers and pharmacists, the shoe store owners, all of them will charge you double what their merchandise is worth."

"But why? The Mission isn't hurting them."

"For these people, there's nothing worse than to have someone treat the Indians like human beings; they've always thought of them as beasts of burden. Or, when they reach the height of their humanitarianism, as slaves."

"Isn't there some way to convince them that they're wrong?"

"I tried to, at first. But it didn't do any good. It's not a question of being reasonable here, it's a matter of interests: the ranch owner who refuses to pay wages to his peons; the pharmacist who wants to go on selling *aceite guapo* and crushed elk's hoof... How can you argue with them? Now we've got open, declared warfare. You'll find out for yourself how many ways the *coletos* have..."

"The *coletos*?"

"That's what they call the people who live in Ciudad Real. As I was saying, how many ways the *coletos* have of being hostile to us."

"Then how can we defend ourselves?"

The Director shrugged.

"There's still no answer to that."

Alicia listened to these revelations with a sense of dread. From that moment on her spirit, which until then had no roots and no center other than her own personal matters, became part of a group — the Mission — uniting with it at this moment in its struggle against the *coletos*.

Alicia moved into the house the Mission rented for its employees. She would be there only temporarily since her destination was the clinic at Oxchuc. But the roads were impassible now because of the rains. Nothing to be done but to wait for drier days to start, for a favorable time to leave. In the meantime there was nothing Alicia had to do. She wandered through offices whose function she never could decipher. There were bundles of paper, files, typewriters, secretaries.

Every once in a while a bell rang urgently. A small disturbance was created whose consequences were never apparent, and then calm reigned again. Yawns, impatient or furtive glances at the clock, an exciting crossword puzzle, some clandestine embroidery. And when they left, all the employees smiled with the satisfaction of having done their job.

Alicia attempted to be likeable. But the *coleta* employees responded to her timid efforts to curry favor with that kind of astute reticence provincial people have. They tried to pry her secrets from her, in case she had any, so they could make fun of her. But they themselves never let slip any information at all.

Feeling disillusioned, Alicia went outside. In the corridor (of an enormous house that had been built with the vague intention of being a seminary or a convent) were the Indians: crowded together, foul-smelling, and identical, waiting for someone to deal with their problems. Land disputes with farmers, labor complaints with hirers. They talked constantly, with animated tones, to each other. Alicia smiled at them, trying to be nice. But they didn't understand the meaning of her gesture.

She finally asked for an appointment with the director. The fact that she wasn't working bothered her, and she wanted to see if she couldn't be useful at something. The director smiled at her, amiably.

"Don't worry. Your turn will come. We don't have a clinic here, so there's nothing a nurse can do. What we need are lawyers."

"They say there are too many of them in Ciudad Real."

"But not one of them will collaborate with us. It would mean being a traitor to their race, to their people."

"Then, why don't you bring one in from Mexico City?"

"Our funds are very limited. We can't hire a competent professional, much less one with some prestige. We have to settle for whatever turns up."

Alicia turned a deep red.

"Sir, I..."

"No, no, I didn't mean to offend you. I myself was just thrown in here to improvise. Of course, I've had other experience: I've been an administrator before. But what's going on here is so different... Anyway, at least we have good intentions. And that's what the Association funding us with money requires."

The director stood up to put an end to the interview.

"As far as you're concerned, don't worry. Go back to your room and rest. There's one thing you'll have to learn from the Indians: that time is of absolutely no importance."

It rained incessantly. Little by little the morning sky would cloud over, and in the afternoon a violent rainstorm would be unleashed to beat down furiously on the tile roofs. Inside her room Alicia brushed her clothing, full of green mold that grew from the humidity.

"When am I going to get out of this place?"

The fact that she couldn't leave Ciudad Real made her feel terrible. One day she caught herself thinking: "the doctor can't leave the clinic either." And from that moment on her anguish grew even greater.

"Don't complain," the director's secretary, Angelina, advised her. "You're better off here than you would be in Oxchuc."

"Is it a very desolate town?"

"It's not even what you would call a town. There are just two or three houses where the *ladinos* live and the rest is a bunch of Indians. A lot of the time there's not even enough food to buy."

"And what does the doctor do? Who takes care of him?"

"Salazar? I imagine he must be in league with the devil. He spends months on end there, and never even looks for an excuse to come to Ciudad Real. Then when he does come, he doesn't talk to a soul. He doesn't even chase after girls. He goes on some total drunks, and he spends the rest of his money on watches. They say he has piles of them."

He's been disappointed in love, Alicia decided. That's what makes Doctor Salazar so cold-hearted. The theory attracted her. It's after an experience like that that men begin to appreciate the importance of a good-hearted woman. And being good-hearted was Alicia's specialty. From that moment on Alicia was able to look at herself in the mirror with less feelings of inferiority.

"So what's Doctor Salazar like? Is he handsome?"

Angelina was pensive for a moment. It had never occurred to her to think of him from that perspective.

"I don't know... he... He has a degree."

For her, and for all the unmarried women in Ciudad Real, that was the important thing. A good catch. What wealthy women could aspire to, the daughters of land-owners, of rich merchants. But not a simple typist. Why should she waste her time thinking about him?

In June the rains let up slightly.

"The roads aren't dry yet," said the director. "But we can't wait any longer. We're going to send medicine and supplies to Oxchuc. This would be a good time for you to go."

Alicia got her bags ready, her heart pounding with happiness. Finally! With her own money, she bought some canned food. And for the ultimate luxury, a can of asparagus. She was certain the doctor would like them.

They left very early the next morning. The streets of Ciudad Real were nearly deserted, but the few pedestrians there were stopped to look, scandalized and amused, to see the spectacle of "a woman who rides a horse like a man." Alicia felt uncomfortable with all those stares aimed at her, for it was the first time she had gotten on a horse, and she felt like she was going to fall off at any moment.

The mule-drivers went in front with the baggage. Alicia took up the rear. The horse realized immediately that its rider had no control over it, and began to walk with reluctance, to suddenly break into a gallop, and to whinny without provocation.

Alicia was pale with fear. The mule-drivers hid their laughter at her ineptness.

And that was just the beginning. The ground was flat at first, but then the hills started to come. Slopes, rocky terrain trenched with unbelievable footpaths. The animals slipped on the enormous stones, they stumbled on the loose sides. Or they got mired down, mud up to their bellies, struggling desperately to move forward.

Alicia looked at her watch. Not more than two hours had gone by. How much longer would it take? She asked them. Every mule-driver gave a different answer.

"There's only a little ways left, and it's all level ground," said one.

"Nothing but rocks, you mean," refuted another.

"It's not even four leagues."

"What a bunch of dreamers! We won't get there till the moon's out."

Meanwhile the road continued to unfold, indifferent to every prediction, its obstacles varying to infinity, imposing new dangers at every step.

It's already getting dark, Alicia observed with surprise. She looked at her watch again. It was three in the afternoon.

"It's the fog," explained a mule-driver.

"It's always foggy out this way. They say it's the fault of Santo Tomás, the patron saint of Oxchuc."

"And why is that, you?"

He's a real prick of a saint, a real 'mother'. First of all, because he didn't believe in Our Lord Jesus Christ..."

"Son of a bee!"

"And so?"

"Well, what they say is one day Santo Tomás threw a rock up at the sky, a rock this big!"

"Ah, what a bunch of crap! You're not going to tell me that the sky fell in on him."

"What else did you expect? Our Lord Jesus Christ wasn't going to lift it up. It serves that son-of-gun right, He said. He knocked it down: so let him lift it up. And from that time on, Santo Tomás tries to do it, every day. But how can he! He gets it up a little ways; but then the sky gets too heavy for him, and it falls down again. Just like right now, for instance. You feel how it's falling down on us. That's what we call fog."

"Aren't you going to light the lamps?" inquired Alicia, apprehensively.

"That won't be necessary, *patrona.* The horses know the way home."

One of the mule-drivers still had a serious theological doubt.

"Hey, listen you. That 'Our Lord Jesus Christ' you just talked about, is he the same one that's got San José under his thumb?"

No one bothered to answer him. There was only derisive laughter.

The rest of the trip was made in the dark. To the already known terrors, Alicia added a thousand imaginary ones: abysses, cliffs, snakes suddenly appearing. Every muscle in her body was tense. Then it began to rain.

It rained all night long. The rain seeped through the oil-skin sleeves, through the straw sombreros, until it soaked the bodies of the travelers who were stiff with cold. Alicia moaned softly each time her horse swayed, each time it stumbled backward. Her warm, salty tears joined with the water streaming down her cheeks.

"Don't fall apart on me, *patrona.* We're almost there!"

Alicia didn't believe these words of consolation. For how many hours now had they been "almost there"? They would never arrive, not anywhere. They were condemned to wander forever in the darkness.

First there was one yellowish, flickering light, far-off in the distance. Then another, and then more, getting nearer. Oxchuc was in sight.

Its nearness made the last few kilometers intolerable. Each step of the horses should have been the last, and it wasn't. In order to get through the next one, Alicia had to make a superhuman effort to overcome her fatigue.

From the Indians' huts, dogs emerged and barked out their hunger, not their ferocity, while here and there a window timidly opened. Alicia couldn't even turn her face to look because her neck was pinched. A few precarious adobe structures began to appear, and then, suddenly and incongruently, they were in front of the vastness of a solid church and a real Municipal Courthouse.

A mule-driver pointed: "There's the clinic."

No matter how she strained, in the shadows Alicia couldn't see a thing. A few moments later they all came to a stop in front of a house the same size and shape as all the others in the town. Its only mark of distinction were some enormous letters, the initials of the Mission.

"This is the clinic?" Alicia asked, disheartened.

"It has a fireplace," boasted one of the mule-drivers.

"You'll need the key to get in. The door's locked. The doctor must have gone out."

"Now we've had it!"

"We'll have to go and find him."

"Let Sabás go; he knows where the doctor's favorite drinking holes are."

"But make him go right now!" urged Alicia.

Her hand flew up to cover her mouth, frightened by the urgent note in her own voice. The only reaction of the mule-drivers was to hurry and obey her.

Alicia needed everyone's help to dismount. She was paralyzed from the cold, and her terror had made her muscles turn completely rigid. Almost dragging her, the mule-drivers laid her down next to the wall of the clinic. There she was sheltered by the tiled overhang of the roof. Curled up to escape the splashes of rain and to hold in what little heat there was in her body, Alicia fell asleep. She didn't awaken until the sun was high in the sky. Someone was shaking her, saying:

"The doctor's here now, *patrona*."

Alicia brushed her hands over her face in consternation. How could she meet him like this, unkempt, a complete mess? My Lord, she couldn't even stand up! She made an effort, but it only resulted in a ridiculous fall. When she lifted her eyes, Alicia saw a man observing her with mocking curiosity.

"So this is the nurse who's come here to take care of my

problems!"

Alicia looked at him with interest. How old could this man be? It was hard to guess what was underneath several weeks' growth of beard, and the bruised look left by a night of insomnia and alcohol. His appearance was as deplorable as that of the just-arrived woman.

Salazar apparently realized that he was being examined because, abruptly, he spun on his heel. He was putting the key in the lock of the clinic door. From the back, thanks to the leather jacket that he wore, he appeared stout.

Alicia caught up with him in the patio. The doctor was counting and inspecting the bundles the mule-drivers had brought. He was grumbling.

"Nothing that we need, as usual. Lab samples, leftovers from the medicines rich people take. Tranquilizers, naturally. Not one vitamin, not one antibiotic. Damn it all to hell!"

Alicia uttered a very soft "Oh!" Salazar wasn't about to bother to beg her pardon. He looked at her severely.

"At least I hope you know how to cook. I've had it up to here with all these filthy cans of sardines."

"Yes, doctor. I brought some provisions too," Alicia exclaimed, delighted at being able to show off her abilities. "...but I'm so dirty right now, I'd like to take a bath before I do anything else."

"A bath?" Salazar repeated, as if someone had just asked for the moon. Then he made a gesture of indifference. "If you want to go to the river, you'll have to travel a league. On foot. And I think I should warn you that at this time of day the water's ice-cold."

The mule-drivers laughed out loud. Trembling with humiliation, Alicia had to make do by moistening a towel and wiping her face with it. She took off her muddy pants and changed into a wrinkled dress. In this attire she made her first incursion into the kitchen.

Whether her cooking met with the doctor's approval, she never knew. She had very little to work with, and to vary the flavor of the dishes and make them look appetizing she managed to do marvels. But Salazar ate in silence, always with an old newspaper spread out in front of him.

"What is it that you're reading?" Alicia ventured to ask him once.

"News of the world," Salazar condescended to reply, the way someone would respond to children or an imbecile.

"But the things it says there happened a long time ago."

"Then it's not news anymore, it's history. Besides, what does time have to do with anything? Nothing ever changes. Everything always stays the same."

Alicia cleared away the dishes. She began to wash them one by one in a metal pan, deliberately making a loud, persistent noise.

"Whenever you tell me, Doctor, I'm ready to help you in the office," Alicia announced a few days later.

Salazar raised his eyes, perturbed by the interruption.

"What? You mean there's nothing left for you to do in the house?"

Alicia didn't feel humiliated at having to do a servant's work. But she was certain that she was needed for other, more important things.

"I've arranged for a girl to come and help me. Everything is taken care of. The only thing we couldn't do was get the fireplace to work. And as cold as it's been..."

"The fireplace is just for decoration. The flue doesn't work."

Alicia wasn't surprised. What else could she expect? But this wasn't what she came for. She folded her hands as though she were waiting for instructions. Salazar noticed her expectant silence, and to break it he insisted:

"So there's nothing else for you to do..."

"Except for your room, Doctor. Since you leave it locked every time you go out..."

"I don't want anybody nosing around in my things."

Alicia had been doing just that, unscrupulously but with no results, ever since she started living in Oxchuc. The only things she found were a pile of scrawled-on papers, dirty clothes (a few, very cheap articles for women) and the fabulous box full of watches of every make and design.

"One of these days when I can watch you, you'll go in and sweep my bedroom. But right now, that's not possible. I'm going out."

"Someone's here to see you, Doctor. Some people came who want a consultation."

"It's not time yet. The clinic is open from ten in the morning till two in the afternoon. No one is seen before or after those hours."

"They're poor people. They say they've come a long way, and they've brought a sick person on a stretcher. I let them into the hallway."

"Well, you did the wrong thing! They're going to infest us with lice and who knows what all kinds of insects. Get them out of there right now."

"But Doctor," protested Alicia, taken aback, "I don't understand..."

"Well, if you don't understand, just follow my orders. And let me warn you: from now on, don't make any decisions unless you have my permission first. I'm the only one who's responsible for the clinic."

"All right, Doctor. But then are you going to just let those people who are waiting for you go away?"

The doctor slammed his newspaper down on the table.

"What do you want? You want me to see the patient? What for? To take his pulse? The medical supplies they sent me are all gone. I don't have a thing to give him. You understand? Nothing."

"At least, talk to them. They'll go back more satisfied if you would say a word to them."

"A word that those Indians wouldn't understand; a word that would lower my reputation, and the Mission's too, because it would just be a lie. If I keep quiet, you think I'm being unjust, which in the end really doesn't matter to me one bit. If I talk to them, I lose their trust. And I need it. You don't know them. In spite of their humble appearance, they didn't come here looking for any favors. They came to demand miracles. They don't think of us as men just the same as them. They want to worship us like gods. Or to destroy us like devils."

Alicia didn't understand his argument. She was ignorant; she hadn't studied for a profession, and she didn't have the years of experience the doctor did in Oxchuc.

"He's a man," she told herself. "He knows what he's doing, and I don't have any right to criticize him."

But she couldn't get rid of the uneasiness she felt whenever she thought about the way Salazar had acted.

December came with its unbearable chill. Shivering, Alicia huddled next to the useless fireplace. Since some time back the doctor had been abandoning his newspaper, and would come over to talk. He spoke animatedly, making broad gestures. Alicia found it difficult to follow his stories. They were confusing, but they were always about the same thing: a student strike from which Salazar still carried scars, because the police had broken it up violently. Then, to erase the bad taste of this memory, he would remember soccer games against the University team.

"Those of us at the Polytechnic fought hard; we had to beat them because they were the boys with money, those rich kids. That was enough to make us believe they were guilty of every evil thing happening in the world. It was all so simple! Now, on the other hand..."

"What about now?" Alicia asked. Because the doctor didn't seem to care to go on.

"Now I know what poor people are like."

He paused for a moment. The expression on his face was one of amused cruelty.

"How stupid! For years I thought I was one of them. And I had to come to Chiapas, to Oxchuc, to find out that I didn't even have the slightest idea of what a poor person really was. And now I can say that I don't like what I've seen."

Alicia didn't understand this way of judging them. It never occurred to her to think of the poor as something to either shun or to approve of because of the trouble they caused. She had always associated them with charity, with alms, with compassion. She was irritated.

"Why?"

"The wealthy exploit us, they abuse us. True. But they allow us the possibility, or to put it better, they make us defend ourselves. The poor, on the other hand, ask; they ask for things endlessly. They want bread, money, attention, sacrifices. They confront us with their misery, and they make us feel like we're the guilty ones."

Salazar was silent for a moment. He seemed to be discovering something.

"You don't suppose that I've become rich too?"

Alicia smiled.

"If you'll forgive me for saying so, it's not very noticeable."

"I mean, inside. When I was a student I got by on Government grants. I slept wherever night caught up with me. I ate when someone invited me to eat. I was always making judgments, I was always condemning everyone else. Now, on the other hand, I have a place to live—not a very comfortable place, but it's secure. A professional position, not a very high one, but with some dignity. I earn a salary. I save money. I buy things. One of these days you'll see the watch collection I have."

"What good are they here, where time doesn't mean anything?"

"That's precisely the point. When a person can buy something absolutely useless, that's when he's really rich."

He began to pace around, taking long strides. Alicia watched him go back and forth, and remembered that next to the watch collection there was a mess of papers, and the dirty, cheap women's clothing. The girl who helped with the housework told her that it belonged to his mistress. How disgusting!

"This complicates things. Sometimes I find it hard to tell the difference between what's good and what's bad. And here, as you're going to find out, nothing is clear. Not clear at all. No matter what a person does, he's always wrong."

Alicia had been wrong. Salazar never responded the way she thought he would. When she had finally come to the conclusion that the doctor was a man who didn't give two cents about his profession, she saw him come in, bursting with happiness.

"Good news, little lady! I just got a box full of vaccine from Ciudad Real. Now let them bring on the epidemics: we've got what we need to take care of them."

Alicia forced a smile. It was difficult for her to get back the enthusiasm she had felt in those first days.

"We'll go out everywhere with a translator and an assistant. You'll come with us: a woman's presence can take away a lot of fear. We'll go from village to village, and there won't be one child left in danger of getting whooping cough or diphtheria or tetanus."

The commission set out early the next morning. The roads were difficult, and they went forward slowly, over the stones and the mud-holes. By noon they had come to a village named Pawinal.

There were some thirty huts spread over a hilly area. When they saw strangers coming, the people of Pawinal ran to hide inside their homes.

"Why are they hiding?" asked Alicia.

"They're afraid. Their *brujos* have warned them not to welcome us. And the priest at Oxchuc has told them the same thing."

"Why?"

"For different reasons. The *brujos* won't put up with any competition. We cure people too. Or, if you like, we also help them to die more easily."

"What about the priest?"

"He doesn't know what to think. First he said we were Protestants. Now he says that we're Communists."

"That's a terrible lie!"

"Do you know what being a Communist really means?"

"Well... no, not really."

"Neither does the priest. He has good intentions when he says it. He thinks we represent a danger, and it's only natural for him to want to defend his flock."

Months earlier Alicia would have exclaimed: "Incredible!" But since she had come to Chiapas the limits of her credulity knew no bounds.

"What are we, Doctor?"

"Didn't they tell you before you came here? People of good will."

"Then, we have to tell them."

"Who?"

"Everyone. These Indians, to start with."

"That's what the translator's been doing ever since we got here. He's been going from house to house, explaining to them that we're not out for any profit for ourselves. That we're not going to exploit them the way other *ladinos* do. That what we want is to help them, to free them from the threat of illness."

"But they won't even listen to him! Why do they run away or shut the door on him or cover their ears?"

"Because they don't understand what's being said to them. Good will! Those words probably don't even exist in their language. And as far as the diseases we want to prevent, they're only remote possibilities. Not only that, but when we vaccinate them they're going to feel sick immediately: they'll have a fever and pain. And why do we say they have to suffer through it? Because of a microbe whose existence they can't believe in since they've never seen it."

"So?"

"So let's go. There's nothing we can do here."

Alicia was too tired to argue. They began the return trip. The translator, a *ladino* from Oxchuc, went in front. He was whistling as though pleased by what had happened. Behind him came the doctor, immersed in his thoughts. The assistant carrying the load. And Alicia, feeling sad.

That evening, after serving dinner, Alicia came over to sit next to the doctor. She needed to talk to him, to hear his thoughts, his justification for actions that were always incomprehensible to her. She asked him:

"Why do you work here?"

"I can give you two answers, one of them idealistic: because everywhere there are people who can be helped. The other is cynical: because they pay me."

"Which one is the truth?"

"Either one of them, depending how you want to see it. I had to work at a lot of jobs, make a lot of sacrifices to get through school.

When I got my degree, all I had was a very modest title: country doctor. With that, I couldn't even open up an office in the poorest little town. My family was terribly worried. I had been their only hope for so many years! I had to do something quick to show them that I was no imposter. Then I learned that an association, a group of humanitarians, as they like to call themselves, was planning to send a doctor to a clinic in Chiapas. That was my chance."

"And have you been here in Oxchuc from the very beginning?"

"There's never been any other clinic."

"What did you think you could do?"

"Wonders. For others, my hands full of gifts. For me, the payment I deserved: fame, money."

Alicia stood up, feeling ashamed. She thought about her own motives: money too, the hope of marriage. How ridiculous! What right did she have to judge him?

"There's a great difference between what you want and what you finally get, isn't there?"

"If we were honest, we'd hand in our resignations."

"Why?"

"Because all this is enough to drive anyone crazy. A clinic that doesn't have any medicine, a doctor that the sick people close their doors on, even a fireplace that doesn't work! It's a joke, Doctor, and I'm not going to put up with it anymore! I want to leave this place!"

"Calm down, Sarah Bernhardt. Getting all worked up won't accomplish anything. The best thing to do is to analyze the situation. This isn't working, I agree. But there must be some reason, the whole structure must be badly planned. If we can find out what's wrong, we can solve everything."

Alicia's eyes opened wide, full of hope. On the doctor's face was a malicious smile.

"But in the meantime we can enjoy all the good things we have here: a guaranteed salary, food and housing. And time to spare. What do you enjoy doing? A lot of women like to knit; some of them read trashy novels, or they just get bored. You won't find an easier life anywhere than you have here."

"I know. There would always be someone watching me so that if I didn't do my job right, they would fire me in a minute."

"I suppose you mean me. But I don't have to explain my conduct to you, since you're just a subordinate. Still, I'm going to soothe your sensitive conscience. Neither one of us is cheating anybody. They didn't send us here to work miracles: to make medicines multiply, or enlighten the minds of the ignorant. They sent us here so we could suffer the cold, the solitude, the abandonment. So that we could share the misery of the Indians, or so that we would be witnesses to it since we can't cure it. It's enough for us to do this, as well as we can, to justify our taking the salary they pay us. And they don't pay us enough, I swear to God!"

The light from the lamp grew weak. Two limpid tears rolled down Alicia's cheeks. The doctor stood up.

"So then, the meeting's adjourned. If you want a tranquilizer, there are plenty of them in the medicine chest."

Alicia remained sitting a while longer, almost in the dark. Then, slowly, she crossed the patio, in the drizzle. Lying in her cot she thought she had lost everything. Why couldn't she keep quiet? What was she defending? Alicia's eyes, dry now, opened wide in the darkness. She was afraid. She wanted to run away, to be somewhere else. In a world that was clean, with good roads, where people were happy and healthy and spoke Spanish. That night she dreamed about her childhood home.

The days went by, monotonously. Once in a while the doctor called Alicia to help him with a patient. She stood by, trembling with shyness, hurrying to carry out his orders — and bungling things so many times! But under Salazar's ironic gaze, these acts lost their meaning, they became an absurd routine.

One night, very late, someone knocked at the door. Alicia awoke, startled, and against the express orders of the doctor, she went to open it.

Two Indians were standing there: fatigue cut their words short. In spite of this, and the clumsy way they expressed themselves in Castilian, Alicia could make out that they had a woman with them who was dying because of a difficult labor. Alicia had them enter. In the light of a candle she could see the wan face of the sick woman. Between the three of them they put her down on Alicia's cot. Then she ran to the kitchen and put on a pot of boiling water.

"What's all the racket?"

It was the doctor (still in his nightclothes) questioning her from his doorway.

She went up to him, pleading.

"It's an emergency, Doctor. I couldn't turn them away."

"Is somebody hurt?"

"A woman's in labor."

"That's odd! They use a *brujo*, or a midwife, to take care of that. The only time they come to the doctor is when they've had an accident."

But while he was talking, Salazar was not idle. He was already back in his room, getting dressed; then he was in the office, sterilizing the instruments he would use. Alicia didn't have to urge him on. The doctor watched over the patient all night long with a solicitude that Alicia joyfully attributed to their conversations. In the early morning hours a little baby boy lay next to its mother, wrapped in improvised swaddling clothes.

Salazar went into the kitchen to ask for a cup of black coffee.

"That woman owes you her life, Doctor. And if they don't name you the baby's godfather, they're really ingrates."

"I don't need any godchildren," protested Salazar. But Alicia's eyes saw the satisfaction he was concealing under his gruff expression.

"The only thing I want to do is to sleep. Don't wake me up unless it's absolutely urgent."

"Don't worry, Doctor."

Alicia told them all to be quiet. The woman's husband and her father-in-law walked through the clinic on tip-toe. The woman rested, with her child in her arms. Alicia went to bed on a divan in the office. Many hours went by.

When Salazar woke up, he went to check on the patient and the newborn baby. Everything was fine. So much so, that he wasn't needed in the clinic. That's why he had decided to go to the social gathering at the Municipal Secretary's place. If they needed him, they could find him there.

"Social gathering!" Alicia muttered to herself. The saloon. Salazar wouldn't come back from his night on the town very soon. Oh, well. She had to trust that they wouldn't have to call him.

During the day Alicia prepared meals for the patient, who was too weak from hemorrhaging. The Indian woman ate timidly, as though she didn't want to show disdain for Alicia's cooking. But she wasn't hungry: she was tired. She fell into a deep sleep, unaware that night was falling. Her child's cries broke through her sleep at dawn, waking her up.

At first the infant's cries were vigorous and angry. But then they changed to a pitiful wail. The Indian woman squeezed her nipples in vain.

The husband and the father-in-law looked at each other with a quick flash of understanding. The woman had undoubtedly been a victim of witchcraft. All women gave birth easily, they can all nurse their babies. Why couldn't she? Could it be that she was guilty of something, and this misfortune was some sort of punishment?

After some minutes of doubt and hesitation, Alicia sent out the girl who helped her with the housework to find the doctor. Salazar came back to the clinic, furious and slightly drunk.

"What's going on here?" he asked as he came inside.

"The woman doesn't have any milk," Alicia said.

"Well, give it some formula. There are baby bottles and cans of condensed milk in the medicine chest."

"But you took the key."

"All right, here it is. Get out what you need. See how much it costs, and have the father pay for it. But get the money before you give them the things, because afterward they won't pay you a cent."

Alicia was dumbfounded. She didn't know that the Mission charged anything. Salazar explained it to her impatiently.

"It's a new rule that I've made. Nothing out of the ordinary. Just a symbolic amount, that's all. Now, that's enough. I deserve some rest too. Or don't you think so?"

Staggering, Salazar went to his room while Alicia added up the costs. For the milk and the bottle, it came to ten pesos.

"I don't have any money," said the younger Indian. The old man affirmed this with a sign that he was telling the truth.

"That's all right," Alicia began to say. "You can give it to me later..."

The most important thing was to satisfy the child's hunger. And if they don't pay me, Alicia said to herself— because you can't depend on these Indians — I'll take the money out of my own pocket. I won't starve because of that little amount.

Salazar's voice boomed out behind her.

"So there's no *takín*, huh? I thought I smelled a trick and that's why I came back. There isn't any money. Well, go to your house and get it. Your baby won't have one drop to drink until you get back."

Alicia turned to the doctor, her eyes wide in disbelief. But instead of taking back what he'd said, Salazar violently grabbed the formula and the baby bottle out of her hand.

"And as for you, Miss Nurse, you are not to give anyone these things without my permission."

The doctor went over to the medicine chest, put the things back in with unsteady movements, and locked it up. Then he confronted the two Indians:

"I've known you for a long time. You can't fool me. Your name is Kuleg, and that means rich."

"But I don't have any money, *ajwalil*."

"Look through your clothes, unwrap your sash. Maybe you're keeping a *cachuco* from Guatemala there, you old man. Paying three or four hundred pesos to a *brujo* doesn't bother you, does it?"

The two Indians lowered their heads and repeated their only phrase:

"We don't have any money."

Salazar shrugged, and without another word he walked to his room. Alicia caught up with him before he could close the door.

"We can't let that baby die of hunger!"

"Does that really depend on us? Over there is the brand new father, and the grandfather. It's up to them to feed it."

"But they don't have money."

"That's a lie! They do. I know so for a fact. The old man owns a maize field and some sheep. The young one could hire himself out to work on the coast, and ask for an advance."

"And in the meantime the child is dying!"

The cries had stopped. Alicia made a grimace of alarm. Salazar smiled.

"It isn't as easy to die as you think it is. He's obviously fallen asleep. But even if that weren't the case, why should you get upset? If that child dies today, he'll escape thirty or forty years of suffering. He'll just end up dying from drunkenness or consumed by fever. Do you think it's worthwhile to save him?"

"I don't care about that! And you don't have any right to decide. Your duty..."

"What is my duty? Suppose I do give a can of milk to Kuleg. It would be enough for a while, three or four days at most. Then he'd have to be given more. I know them, Alicia, they're leeches, like all Indians, like all poor people. And the clinic has barely enough to keep itself going. It can't afford the luxury of nursing children."

"Doctor, I beg you...!"

Alicia wasn't listening to the man's arguments. She only wanted to run to the newborn baby and put a bottle full of warm milk to its mouth.

"What a good example we'd be setting for them! Today it's Kuleg who makes fools of us, because he has money, I know so for a fact! Tomorrow it will be someone else. And when we've given out all the medicine, then what? We won't have one cent to buy any more. And besides that, we won't have a single customer left. Because they don't value what they get without paying for it. The *brujo* can do more than we can because he costs more!"

Alicia covered her ears. Abruptly, she left Salazar. In the patio she found the two Kulegs, sitting down, smoking. She went over to the young one.

"I'm going to give you the money, but don't tell anyone, just run and hand it to the doctor. Hurry, before it's too late."

Alicia had knelt down, and was speaking quickly. She took out some coins that the two Indians looked at, without making the slightest gesture of taking them.

"The *pukuj* is eating up my child."

This explanation, so simple, made any action superfluous. Alicia turned to the old man in supplication. But he was looking back at her with a stupefied gaze that foreign words, incoherent gestures, were unable to penetrate.

Alicia got up in dismay and went to her room. The sick woman was sitting on the edge of the cot, braiding her hair. She was still pale, but there was no sign of anxiety on her face. The infant was asleep, sucking on its entire hand.

Alicia began talking quickly. She shook the Indian woman by the shoulders, as though to awaken her. She did not protest, and she agreed docilely to everything. She did not understand what they were asking of her. But she held back in order to obey only her husband.

Alicia left the room and went into the office. She attempted to force open the door to the medicine cabinet for a long while, but the lock would not give way. And she did not have the strength to break it.

Drained by a sleepless night and by the things she had witnessed but not been able to change, Alicia sat down on the ground, under the eaves of the patio. In that manner the hours went by. Occasionally the hoarse cries of the child broke through the silence. Then everything would become peaceful again.

When night fell, the old man, his son, and the woman holding a small corpse in her arms left the clinic. Salazar had still not woken up.

When he did wake up, Alicia was packing her suitcases. Yawning, lost in some thought, Salazar didn't say a word about what had happened.

"I've told the director of the Mission many times: it's not enough to put hot cloths on a wound. You have to yank the problem out by the roots. Remember what you and I were talking about the other night? You have to know what the real problem is. And finally, I've figured it out. The real problem is to educate the Indians. We have to teach them that the doctor and the clinic are necessities. They already know that necessities cost money; if we give them everything, they don't appreciate what they get. They're really prone to evil ways. I know them, damned if I don't. I've lived among them for years. Alone, like a dog. With no one I can talk to. And afraid. Afraid of the vengeance of the *brujos*, of people who are angry because someone was sick and I wasn't able to save him. How could they expect me to save him? They bring him to me when it's too late. They don't have any gratitude. It's always someone else who gets the credit: a saint, a *brujo*. But they're cowards, they can only kill someone by treachery. They never show their faces, they won't look you straight in the eye. And with no one I can talk to. The *ladinos* in Oxchuc are a bunch of schemers, they're envious. You have to be careful of them too, because you never know when they'll put a gun to your head. You've got to have guts to put up with this. Before you came I always did my own cooking because I was afraid they might poison me. It's not fair. You study for a profession, you burn the midnight oil for years. No fun, no women, no nothing. And your family sacrificing so you can get a degree. Your reward will come later. And then they send you out here to rot away. Sure, I could leave whenever I want to. I'm a very good doctor, I could find a better job anywhere... It would be better for me if I did. I need to see people, I need to meet someone I can talk to, someone I can explain things to... Because I've discovered something, something very important. It's not enough to have good intentions; what's important is education. Education. These Indians don't understand a thing and someone has to start teaching them... Then you come here, with your fussiness, acting like a nun, and you think it's easy to look down on me because I get drunk once in a while and because you've found out that I have a mistress and because..."

Alicia didn't answer. The sobs were choking her.

"Sometimes I wind all my watches at the same time. It's nice to hear them all running. They don't stop, never ever."

Suddenly Salazar went over and took Alicia by the shoulders.

"What do you think is worth more? The life of that little boy, or of all the rest of them? Kuleg will tell them what happened. We taught them a lesson, and what a lesson! Now the Indians will know that you can't fool around with the clinic in Oxchuc. They'll start coming—they sure will!—and with money in their hands. We'll be able to buy medicine, all kinds of medicine..."

Salazar was waving his arms. Alicia drew back from him, and when she finished putting in her clothes, she closed the suitcase. Outside, it was raining.

The Gift, Refused

First of all, let me introduce myself. My name is José Antonio Romero, and I'm an anthropologist. Yes, in a certain sense, anthropology is a rather new field of study at the University. The first instructors had to improvise, and in all the confusion there was an opportunity for some undesirable elements to filter in, but little by little they've been weeded out. Now we, the new ones, are struggling to raise our School to a position of respect. We even took the battle to the Senate of our Republic when they discussed the matter of professional accreditation.

But I'm getting off the track. What I wanted to talk to you about wasn't that, but rather a very curious incident that happened to me in Ciudad Real, where I work.

As you know, there's an Indian Aid Mission in Ciudad Real. At first it was funded and supported with private contributions, but since then it's passed into the hands of the Government.

I'm just one of many skilled workers there, and my duties are rather varied. I'm the chief cook and bottle-washer, as the saying goes. I investigate cases, I serve as intermediary for conflicts between towns, I've even acted important in the role of a marriage-broker. Of course, I can't just sit in my office and wait for people to come to me. I've got to take the bull by the horns, and go looking for whatever problems are out there. In this sort of situation a car is absolutely indispensable. Lord, what I went through to get one! Everyone, the doctors, teachers, engineers, were all asking for the exact same thing. So anyway, we took care of it somehow. Now, at least for a few days a week, I have a jeep at my disposal.

The jeep and I have come to an understanding. I know all its little idiosyncrasies, and I've even figured out how far it can be pushed. I've discovered that it works better out on the highway (well, anyway, what we call a "highway" in Chiapas) than in town.

Because there, the traffic is a mess. Either there are no stoplights or they don't work right, and nobody pays any attention to them. The *coletos* will walk right down the middle of the road without a care in the world, talking away and laughing, as if sidewalks didn't even exist. You want to blow your horn? Well, go right ahead, if you feel like wasting your time. The pedestrian won't even turn to see what's going on, much less move over to let you pass.

But the other day something very strange happened to me, and that's what I want to tell you about. I was coming back from the Navenchauc village, in my jeep, and I was going down the Calle Real de Guadalupe, where the Indians and *ladinos* do business together. I couldn't go any faster than ten kilometers an hour, caught in the middle of all that mess, and the people were taking their own sweet time haggling over prices, or staggering under the load of huge packages filled with goods that they were carrying. I just said ten kilometers, but actually at times my speedometer needle didn't move off of zero.

Going that slow put me in a bad mood, even though I was really in no hurry, in fact far from it. Then, suddenly, from out of nowhere a little Indian girl about twelve years old deliberately darts right out in front of the jeep. I managed to put on my brakes, and I just brushed her a little with my bumper. But I got out, boiling mad, letting loose a lot of curse words. I'm not going to hold anything back from you, even if I'm ashamed of it. I don't usually act that way, but this time I swore like any of the *ladinos* in Ciudad Real.

The little girl listened to me, whimpering away, hypocritically rubbing her eyes where there wasn't even a trace of a tear. I felt sorry for her and, even with all my convictions against giving out charity and about the uselessness of such individual acts, and in spite of the fact that I detest sentimentality, I took out a coin amid the mocking comments of all the busybodies who were gathering around.

The little girl wouldn't take the money, but she grabbed my sleeve and tried to lead me to a place whose name I couldn't make out. The busybodies began to laugh, of course, and they started calling out suggestive remarks, but I didn't pay any attention to them and I followed her.

Now don't get me wrong. I didn't think for a minute that this was any kind of romantic liaison, because if that's what it had been, I wouldn't have been interested. I'm young, I'm not married, and sometimes, in these poor villages, a man's need for a woman is overwhelming. But I work for an Institution, and we have something called professional ethics which I respect. Besides, why not admit it? My tastes are a little more demanding.

Well, anyway, to make a long story short, we got to one of the side streets that lead into the Calle de Guadalupe, and that's where I find a woman, an Indian, lying on the ground, apparently unconscious, with a new-born baby in her arms.

The girl pointed to her, and said who knows what in her dialect. Unfortunately, I still haven't learned it, because besides the fact that my field is social anthropology and not linguistics, I haven't been in Chiapas for very long. So I drew a complete blank.

When I bent over the woman I had to stifle an impulse to cover up my nose with a handkerchief. There was an odor coming from her that... I don't quite know how to describe it. It was very strong, very pungent, and absolutely repulsive. It wasn't just the smell of a person who's filthy, although the woman was filthy enough and her wool jacket was soaked with sweat. It was something more intimate, more... How can I put it? More organic.

Instinctively (I don't know any more about medicine than anybody else), I took her pulse. And the quickness of it, its wild beating, startled me. If that was any indication, the woman was seriously ill. I didn't hesitate one more minute. I went to get the jeep so I could drive her to the Mission clinic.

The little girl didn't leave our side for a moment. She picked up the little baby, who was crying desperately, and she made sure that even if the sick woman wasn't all that comfortable in the back of the jeep, at least she was secured in the seat.

When I pulled up at the Mission, you can imagine the commotion we created: everyone came running out to see what all the fuss was about. But they had to just stay curious because I couldn't tell them any more than what I've told you.

After he had examined her, the doctor at the clinic said that the woman had puerperal fever. And no wonder! Her baby had been born in who knows what kind of filthy conditions, and now she was paying the price with an infection that had her right at death's door.

It really got to me. I had a sort of vacation coming right about then, and I decided to spend all my time with these people who had turned to me when they were in trouble.

When the antibiotics from the pharmacy at the Mission were gone, I went to buy them myself in Ciudad Real just to save all the paperwork, and what I couldn't find there I went all the way to Tuxtla to get. Where did the money come from? It came right out of my own pocket. If I'm telling you all this, it's not because I'm fishing for compliments that I don't care about in the least, it's just that I said I wouldn't hide anything from you. Why would I deserve praise, anyway? I make a good living, I'm a bachelor, and in these towns there's not much to buy. I've got some money in savings. What I wanted was for the woman to get better.

While the penicillin was starting to work, the little girl walked around the corridors of the clinic with the baby in her arms. That little stinker never stopped his bleating. And with good reason: he was hungry! They gave him baby formula, and the wives of some of the employees of the Mission (good women, if you found their soft spot) brought diapers and talcum powder and all that sort of thing for the kid.

Little by little, those of us who lived at the Mission began to feel attached to that family. We heard about their problems down to the most minute detail, thanks to a servant who did the translating from Tzeltal to Spanish, because right about that time the linguist was off on a lecture tour.

It turned out that the sick woman, whose name was Manuela, had become a widow just a few months after she'd gotten pregnant. Then the owner of the land that her dead husband was renting pulled the rug right out from under her. He claimed that the peon had some debts that he'd never paid back: loans of money and goods, advances, a complete mess that the widow was left to untangle.

Manuela ran away from there and went to live with her relatives. But being pregnant the way she was, it was hard for her to work in the maize fields. Besides that, the harvests had been poor for the last few years, and all the villages were grumbling about how scarce food was.

So what was the poor woman to do? The only thing she could think of was to go down to Ciudad Real and see if she could find a job as a maid. Now just stop and think for a minute: Manuela a maid! This was a woman who didn't know how to cook anything except beans, who wasn't capable of doing the shopping, who didn't even understand Spanish. And to top it all off, she had a baby on the way.

After she had nearly worn herself out looking, Manuela finally found a position at an inn for muledrivers that a certain Doña Prájeda ruled over. This woman had the reputation all over the neighborhood of making whoever had the misfortune of serving her break their backs with all the work she gave them.

Well, that's where my lucky Manuela ended up. Since her pregnancy was so far along, she did her work with the help of her oldest child, Marta, who was a very clever, lively young girl.

Somehow together they managed to please the *patrona*, who, I learned later, had her eye on Marta, intending to sell her to the first man who asked for her.

No matter how she may deny it now, Doña Prájeda had to have known about Manuela's condition when she took her on. But when the time came for the baby to be born, she pretended to be surprised, raised the roof, said that her inn was no shelter, and made arrangements to have her servant taken to the County Hospital.

Poor Manuela cried her eyes out. Just think about it, who knows what her imagination had conjured up about the sort of place a hospital was. A kind of jail, a place for penitence and punishment. Finally, with all her begging, the *patrona* relented and let her give birth at the house.

Now, Doña Prájeda is one of those people who never do anybody a favor all the way. Just so Manuela wouldn't bother anyone with her screams, she stuck her out in the stable. There, in the manure and with all the flies and God knows how many other filthy things, the Indian woman had her child and came down with the fever that she had when I brought her in.

As soon as the first symptoms of illness began to appear, the *patrona* had an absolute fit and without a second thought, she threw the whole family right out into the street. Who knows how long they would have been there if some charitable soul hadn't felt sorry for them and advised Marta to go to the Mission for help, since her mother was so terrified of the County Hospital.

Marta didn't even know where the Mission was, but when they saw a jeep with our insignia passing by, someone gave her a shove so that I would stop.

If we forget about the fright of it all and the tongue-lashing I gave her, the ruse didn't turn out too badly for them, because in the Mission we not only cured Manuela but also concerned ourselves with what would happen to her and her children after they discharged her from the clinic.

Manuela was too weak to work, and Marta was more or less at the age where she could learn. So why not put her in the boarding school of the Mission? They teach them skills there, the rudiments of reading and writing, the manners and constraints of civilized people. And after their apprenticeship, they can go back to their own villages with a job, with a decent salary, and with a new sense of dignity.

That's what we suggested to Manuela, thinking that she would welcome the idea with open arms. But the Indian woman's only response was to press her baby more tightly to her breast. She wouldn't answer.

We were surprised at her reaction, but discussing it among the anthropologists, we figured out that what was bothering Manuela was the money her daughter earned from working, money she was counting on to be able to support herself.

You can appreciate the fact that it was nothing extraordinary, really just a few cents, and for me, just like for anybody, that monthly expense wouldn't be any sacrifice at all. I went to the woman to suggest the arrangement, and I explained the matter very clearly to the interpreter.

"She says that if you want to buy her daughter to make her your mistress, she wants a drinking jug and two measures of corn in return. You can't have her for less."

Perhaps it might have been more practical to accept those terms that seemed so normal and innocent to Manuela, because they were the customs of her race. But I insisted on trying to show her, both for the sake of the Mission and my own sake too, that our intentions weren't like those of some *ladino* in Ciudad Real. We didn't want to degrade them or exploit them, we wanted to give her daughter a chance to get an education and to have a better life. It was useless. Manuela wouldn't quit with that business of the drinking jug and the corn, and when she saw how insistent I was, she wanted a measure of beans as well.

I decided just to leave her alone. They continued to take care of her and her children at the clinic, feeding them and spraying their heads with DDT because they were swarming with lice.

But I didn't give up on the idea. It hurt my conscience to see a young girl as bright as Marta grow up depending on the mercy of God to get by, to have her end up in who knows what kind of miserable situation.

Someone suggested to me that my best chance to win over the mother's confidence was through religion. Being a godparent is a spiritual relationship that the Indians really respect. The new born baby hadn't been baptized, so why not try to convince Manuela, little by little, to make me her son's godfather?

I began by buying toys for the little one: a tambourine, amber to guard against the evil eye. I tried to be there whenever the nurse came to give him a bath, and I even learned to change his diapers without doing too much damage.

Manuela allowed me to do these things, but she was uneasy about it, and she had misgivings that her smiles couldn't hide. She only breathed easily when the baby was back in her own lap again.

Despite all this, I really thought I was gaining ground, and one day I decided that the time had come to bring up the matter of the baptism.

After the indispensable beating around the bush, the interpreter told her that the baby couldn't go on living like a little animal, without a name and without the sacrament of baptism. I watched as Manuela agreed docilely with our words, and even supported them with affirmative gestures and emphatic exclamations. I thought the whole thing was settled.

But when it came time to choose a godparent, Manuela wouldn't let us go on. That was something she had thought about right from the start, and there was no arguing with her.

"Who?" the translator asked.

I stepped a few steps away to allow the sick woman to speak freely.

"Doña Prájeda," answered the Indian woman in her halting speech.

I couldn't contain myself, and grabbing hold of the bars of the bed, I shook it angrily.

"Doña Prájeda?" I repeated incredulously.

The woman who sent you to the stable so you could give birth to your child in all that filth? The woman who threw you out into the street when you most needed her help and her kindness? The woman who hasn't stopped by the Mission even once to ask if you were dead or alive?

"Doña Prájeda is my *patrona*," Manuela answered seriously. "We haven't broken our agreement. I'm still under her control."

To make a long story short, the discussion went on for hours, and it was impossible for Manuela and I to come to an agreement. I left the clinic, cursing a blue streak, and swearing never again to get myself involved in something that was none of my business.

A few days later Manuela left the clinic with her children, completely healthy again. She went back to work for Doña Prájeda, of course.

Sometimes I see her in the street, and she avoids looking at me directly. But not as though she's ashamed or has any regrets. Instead, it's as if she's afraid I'm going to bring her some harm.

No, please, don't call Manuela ungrateful, or contemptible, or stupid. Don't reach the conclusion, just to avoid your own responsibility, that Indians are a hopeless cause. Her attitude is completely understandable. She can't distinguish between one *caxlán* and another. We're all alike to her. When one of them does something brutal to her she expects it, she knows what she's supposed to do. But when another one is kind to her and gives her something without demanding anything in return, she doesn't understand. That's outside the rules everyone goes by in Ciudad Real. She's afraid that the trap may be even more dangerous, and she defends herself the only way she knows how: by running away.

I know all this; and I know too that if we work hard— those of us at the Mission and everyone else—someday things will be different.

But meanwhile, Manuela, Marta... What will become of them? What I want you to tell me is this: did I, as a professional, as a man, do something wrong? There must have been something. Something I didn't know how to give them.

Arthur Smith Finds Salvation

"a good man,
in the best sense of the word."
—Antonio Machado

As the helicopter flew over the mountain ridge (sharp peaks, precipices, something small moving in the foliage), Arthur Smith thought about how the world, most definitely, was well made. At least with regard to what you could see at first glance, in nature, in its external appearance, anyone wagering that it was beautiful would win. These combinations of colors he had before him now, for example. Every single element, blue, green, somber purple, was of a clarity and a purity that was impossible to confuse with the others, in spite of their proximity and even their blending.

Confusion results from a careless, quick glance. When the eye pauses, it can be discerning, and it can distinguish with exactness.

Arthur Smith took out a black, leather-bound notebook and quickly jotted down some figures and notes to record his thoughts. They might come in handy later on. Observations of this kind, so simple and taken from daily life, are the ones that people like, and that win them over.

People, for Arthur Smith, were the common people, humble in their ignorance, to whom the Lord had spoken in parables. The parables' meanings, so transparent and yet so multivalent, revealed themselves in secret to each heart, and came forth with absolute clarity in each individual circumstance. Sometimes, one meaning seemed to contradict another, or to take away its validity. But that was simply a consequence of the irremediable limitations of the human intellect ("Reason, proud to proclaim its conquests, blind to its errors, incapable of going beyond its barriers," he wrote) which always finds the designs and ways of God inscrutable.

The helicopter, handled capably and steadily (how could it be otherwise, if the pilot was an American?), began to descend. A large clearing suddenly appeared in the pine forest where not only a craft as small as the one carrying Arthur, but even large, powerful airplanes could land.

Arthur Smith closed his black, leather-bound notebook, and put it away. He couldn't go on writing with all this reeling back and forth, and then the light, intermittent bouncing of the helicopter's wheels as they touched ground.

Upon landing, the pilot turned to Arthur—his only passenger—with a wide smile of good toothpaste and chlorophyll gum that expressed both his satisfaction at having completed his mission, and his happiness at having had an audience.

"We're not too badly situated here, as you can see," the pilot remarked, as he looked around. Several large hangars—empty at the moment—and a small control tower made up the immediate panorama. Behind them stood a thick grove of pine trees.

The radio transmission operator emerged from the tower, exuberant, to greet his compatriots.

With a natural deference he went over to Arthur Smith first, and gave him a hearty handshake and a short welcome on behalf of Pastor Williams, unable to be there because of the pressing duties of his ministry. Then his conversation slid, as fluid and zestful as if it had never been interrupted, over to the pilot. They talked about mechanical things, about a shipment they were all waiting for impatiently, and, when the two of them thought Smith wasn't listening, about some more profane matters. The pilot revealed a very nice surprise to the radio technician: in his baggage he had brought a magnificent collection of French postcards.

Arthur, who tried to distract himself by kicking small pebbles along the road, couldn't avoid getting the meaning of what they were whispering about. He blushed down to the roots of his hair, and clenched his fists. How could these bastards...? But long training in the mastery of his impulses made the symptoms of anger disappear. After all, he reflected, these two men walking ahead of him formed a part of the "flock of lost sheep." They had been touched by no special grace, they had been singled out for no special mission. From their clay, a worthless vessel was molded. On the other hand, he, Arthur... he sighed in deep satisfaction. He was finally in the place where he belonged, and his place was that of the elect. He had arrived at his destiny.

Now he remembered the years of doubts, of postponement. "Lord, could I be worthy of serving You?" And he was never sure if the question was one of humility, or cowardice.

The world tempted him, that world the ancients had considered dangerous, not even imagining the extremes of seductiveness it would finally reach. All the devices for living comfortably and with ease; all the instruments for providing pleasure; all the colors and sounds for bewildering the senses. Everything within reach of every man. "Buy now, pay later." And hordes of people rushed in, their hands anxious to grab whatever they could, at any price. And every one of them pushing the others aside to get there first, needing to be unique. You had to separate yourself from the crowd, to be original, eccentric, to become famous. It didn't matter how you did it. "I married a convict of Sing-Sing." "I taught an ostrich how to do tricks." "I ate two-hundred hamburgers in three hours."

Fame meant money. And money... Well, come on! Who doesn't know the meaning of money? Arthur Smith wanted both things, but in a passive, abstract way. If someone had come along and offered them to him, he wouldn't have turned them down. But to go chasing after them, to clear a path by pushing everyone else aside... No, evidently he wasn't made of the same mettle as the pioneers, or aggressive executive types. And then Arthur justified himself by thinking how the world was the vanity of vanities, and better to lose it, as long as his soul was saved.

But even these were remote considerations. They only took on a sense of reality when his mother died. That cancer... My God! Was there anything that could erase the repugnant odor of flesh rotting slowly away, day after day? And the screams of pain. Where could the spirit take refuge in those poor bodies, tortured by illness and treatments, stupefied with pain-killers? And yet, the last moment of agony had been so luminous that Arthur Smith was left in amazement. His mother had looked at him with a wide, moist look that could have encompassed the heavens. A look of reconciliation, of certainty that all was in order and was good, at peace.

From that moment on, Arthur began attending more frequently the church his mother had belonged to: the Protestant denomination of the Brethren of Christ.

Arthur felt good inside a solemn building without graven images, among people with a benevolent air about them, who wore hats that were slightly old-fashioned.

In the sermons that he heard, there was something (a similarity to his mother's words?) that caused him to relive his childhood. The figure of Christ always appeared, resplendent, full of goodness and tenderness. His acts were simple. He always consoled the sad, pardoned the sinners, softened the hard of heart. It was easy to be good in those days. As easy as walking on water.

Arthur Smith made a few tentative attempts to do good works in his parish. But his enterprising nature (after all, Arthur was an American too) wasn't satisfied with simply giving charity from time to time to some beggar, whose punctual appearance he couldn't even count on. Beyond that, he detested visiting the slums of his town. There was so much prostitution there (bars, hotels rented by the hour, tramps) that their misery could only be considered a divine punishment, which he had no right to excuse.

Arthur Smith sought out the opinion of several people more knowledgeable than he, and they all advised him to join a vast, powerful Organization whose branches operated in the most isolated and primitive regions of Latin America.

The Organization used an unpronounceable acronym for its name, in an attempt to combine the initials of all the private clubs that contributed to its support and all the religious sects that lent their collaboration.

When Arthur Smith presented himself at the recruitment office of the Organization, they required only two things of him: that he be a Christian, and that he learn some specialty useful for the place where his services would be needed.

Arthur Smith enrolled in an intensive course on Mayan dialects, specializing in Tzeltal, since the place he had chosen as his destination was an encampment called Ah-tún in the highlands of Chiapas, in the southern region of the Republic of Mexico.

His studies did not make him neglect his moral discipline, but rather strengthened it. As long as he was a bachelor (and he hadn't the slightest intention of changing that), he had to practice sexual abstinence. It wasn't always possible for him to do so. But he took consolation in reading and re-reading that passage where it is affirmed that the flesh is weak, and that a righteous man falls seventy times each day.

As for other sins, they didn't bother him much. Since the Organization took care of his lodging, clothing, meals, course tuition and a small allowance for incidental expenses, greed had disappeared from his horizon. His personal vanity was satisfied. And wasn't it legitimate for Arthur to feel that way to a small degree, when he had been able to follow the narrow path and was prepared to sacrifice himself in order to save others?

Arthur Smith received a diploma recognizing his proficiency in the pre-Hispanic languages of Mesoamerica, and with it neatly rolled up inside his suitcase, he departed for the camp at Ah-tún.

It was a quick trip, using the most modern means of transportation. Jet airplanes across the United States. A four engine plane from Mexico City to the capital of Chiapas. And a helicopter from Tuxtla Gutiérrez to Ah-tún.

At first glance, it would seem that the trip went downhill in the process. But while Arthur Smith was soaring through the air, swift and sure, others less privileged than he (functionaries of the Indian Aid Mission, private citizens, the natives) had to cross the mountain ranges of Chiapas in unbelievable jeeps, on the backs of beasts or of patient Indians, or on foot.

The privilege of traveling by helicopter did not weaken Arthur's humility, but instead strengthened his sense of being on the "side of good." His religion was the true one, his race was superior, his country was powerful. God, Arthur solemnly affirmed, didn't need human souls to make the journey from this world to the one beyond in order to make manifest His preferences or to reward certain types of behavior with success, because His justice was swift, besides being infallible and unalterable.

But, of course, being on the "side of good" could in no way be considered a simple accident. These events had been the object of meditations by Divine intelligence for a long time, since the beginning of creation. So therefore it was fitting that the man, Arthur Smith, should in some way return the favors he had received.

(The word "favor" was not one Arthur preferred, since it could be interpreted as a diminishing of personal merit. Unfortunately, merit existed in direct relation to responsibility, and the latter could bring guilt as a consequence, which in turn led to punishment. So Arthur Smith resigned himself to leaving things the way he had found them.)

As we were saying then, Arthur Smith had received innumerable favors from Providence: that of understanding and accepting Revelation; that of practicing and enforcing morality; that of displaying citizenship of the most respected country in the world; that of sporting the proper color of skin; that of handling a currency that was always worth more than any other.

So then, how could he make the investment that Providence had put into him yield the greatest possible benefits? He could become a prosperous businessman. In his religion there was not a single commandment against this, and the laws of his country offered him all sorts of opportunities. However (in spite of the many autobiographies of millionaires who had begun their careers shining shoes), the competition was extremely stiff.

So Arthur Smith settled for a bureaucratic job. But most of those positions were held by people who had an inexcusable tendency toward immorality. And as soon as any vacancy appeared, the same crowd that gathered at the entrances of subways and elevators appeared immediately to fill it.

There were other means: luck, for example. But the statistics consistently indicated that all the petroleum deposits had already been discovered, and the same held true for mines of precious metals or those new substances that modern industry demanded, in ever-increasing quantities, for its development.

Arthur discarded the idea of becoming an inventor after leafing melancholically through the files of the Patent Office.

One opportunity did arise intermittently: war. But Arthur Smith did not have a particularly combative spirit. The God of the Army established communication with him from time to time, and even then His commandments were more ambiguous than they were imperative. And yet, when he saw enormous posters appear on all the walls and pillars of the city that made a dramatic call to his heroism to save the sacred patrimony of Liberty, Democracy and Human Dignity being threatened by an implacable enemy on a remote island in the Pacific, Arthur Smith ran quickly to the recruiting office, but with feet so flat that his application was turned down.

Mama and her small widow's pension helped him get through difficult years when his work as a traveling salesman exposed him to violent attacks by ferocious dogs, the mischief of disrespectful boys, and doors slammed by disheveled housewives.

Moreover, his eloquence—which would have shone splendidly from a pulpit, commenting passages from the Gospels—became an ineffectual stammer when he had to praise the all-encompassing virtues of a detergent, of a can-opener that turned into the most unexpected kind of utensil, of a multi-purpose brush.

"Your problem," his mother advised him with a clarity that comes only from love, "is that you have no faith."

And that was exactly it. Arthur could not have faith in something as flimsy as a brush; faith was something he reserved for more lofty ideals. He believed in the promises of politicians; he trusted the honesty of major-league baseball managers; he would have put his hand in the fire to swear to the encyclopedic knowledge of the participants on television quiz shows.

When those ideals collapsed for one reason or another, Arthur Smith's faith turned, completely and fervently, toward the only illusion that publicity could not fabricate or undo at its whim: toward God.

It was faith in God that had now moved Arthur into unexplored regions, where tribes of savage Indians awaited the message of light and redemption.

"There's the Ah-tún camp," announced the radio technician as he pointed out a group of small, wooden houses, painted in vibrant colors. On the only street, implacably straight and impeccably paved, healthy, blond children went about riding bicycles, or atop roller-skates. The pilot asked where the nearest soda-fountain was. It was a joke that he and his friend, the radio technician, invariably replayed. But Arthur Smith didn't know that, and he glowered at them both with a disapproving scowl. The first thing they needed to find out, he said, was the location of the church. As Christians, it was their duty to go there and give thanks to the Lord for having brought them safely to the end of their journey.

The radio technician seemed a little ashamed to answer. The church, he said, was a considerable distance away, in the thick of the jungle. (He called anything that was a field a jungle, without distinguishing those small nuances that make a plain neither forest nor desert.)

The wisest course for the newcomers, he added, would be to rest a while. He would take them to the guest house where Arthur would be staying in one of the rooms, because it was his understanding that he was a bachelor and wouldn't need a house. As for the pilot, he knew only too well where his lair was.

"In the meantime, I'll have them fix you something to drink."

Arthur didn't think it very hospitable for the housewives not to come out to meet him. After all, his position as a linguist held a certain importance, and besides, it's always nice to pay your respects to a fellow compatriot when you're in a foreign land. Some childhood memory had made him dream about apple pies just coming out of the oven. But in the air you could only sense a vague odor of disinfectant. The kitchens were closed up and silent. This was the hour when the women were listening to a terribly complicated episode in which a seductive, dark and despicable man was about to make the ingenuous heiress to fall into his net, from which she would be saved at the very last moment by the loyalty of the administrator of her dead father's estate. The administrator was a young blond man, freckle-faced and plain, who had always loved her, though he had never dared to confess it.

Pastor Williams returned at dusk. Thin, delicious lines of smoke were now escaping from the kitchens, and the electricity generator produced a continuous, lulling buzz.

Arthur and Williams met in the sitting room of the guest house. An immediate, congenial current went between them as they discovered startling coincidences in their personal tastes. They both preferred Coca-Cola over any other brand of bottled soft-drink, and mild rather than strong tobacco. Their conversation, which had begun so auspiciously, could not continue for long because the pilot needed Pastor Williams to sign the inventory list for the items he had transported: several rolls of 16-millimeter film, some cases of antibiotics, and a package of copies of the New Testament, along with other books and magazines. He couldn't wait because he was taking off for Tuxtla at dawn the next day.

There were also some definite plans for the next day for Arthur. Someone would take him through the camp so that he could admire its facilities: a swimming pool with tepid water (the way the climate required), an auditorium where lectures were given, movies were shown, and even amateur plays were presented. At dinner time, it would be his pleasure to accept the invitation of Pastor Williams and his family to dine with them.

Mrs. Williams—middle aged with two children, her beauty fading without a struggle—seemed delighted by Arthur's visit. Anything new in this land of exile, she declared without thinking that her words might be misinterpreted as rude, became exciting. So exciting that this was the first time in months she had personally taken a hand in the planning of the menu, and even in the preparation of the dishes. Because the Indian cooks, like all the rest of the servants that her husband had provided her with, were more of a nuisance than a help.

"They're stupid, dirty, stubborn hypocrites..."

"Liz, please," the Pastor cut her off, handing her a tray full of drinks. "Remember, you promised to be patient."

Liz smiled, her eyes nearly welling with tears, and drank down most of her glass in one swallow.

"I'll go see if dinner is ready," she said.

And she left the room with stiff, deliberately noisy steps.

The three of them sat at the table. The children, Liz explained, were outside. And, well, she hoped nobody would complain about that. The children just interrupt adult conversations, asking silly questions and spilling things on the tablecloth.

"That's because of the way they're brought up," said Pastor Williams, peevishly.

"And am I the only one who's supposed to be raising them? You're always off somewhere. And the only examples the children get around here are bad ones. The other day I found Ralph crying because he didn't have lice like all the natives."

Liz's cheeks were flushed. At that moment an Indian woman came in, carrying a platter of meat which she clumsily deposited next to the Pastor.

"Haven't I told you a thousand times that I'm the one who's supposed to serve the meal?"

The angry voice belonged to Liz. The Indian woman lowered her eyelids, and smiling without comprehension, went back into the kitchen, her bare feet hardly touching the floor.

"Did you see that?" Liz complained to the Pastor, to Arthur, to anyone. "And they still expect the children to be well brought up."

"Dear, our guest isn't interested in domestic problems."

"Please excuse me, Mr. Smith! And besides, how absurd to waste time on silly little things like this when there are so many interesting things to talk about."

Liz was talking as though she was afraid that some invisible operator, like on a telephone, was going to cut her off. Quickly, anxiously. What was New York like? Was it really as enormous as everyone said? She had never been there, nor had she been to Hollywood, Florida, Las Vegas, or Niagara Falls. On the other hand, she said ironically, looking at her husband, she had been to Ah-tún.

"Bring our coffee, please."

Outside on the porch, with the cut-glass coffeepot in front of them, each with a lighted cigarette of the same brand, Arthur and Williams sat alone.

"I think Liz needs a vacation. She's been out here too long."

He did not bring her up again. Arthur expected that now the Pastor would spell out what duties he would assign to him at the camp. But it didn't turn out that way. He simply recommended that Arthur become acquainted with the place, that he get to know the others.

Little by little, Arthur came to know each of his companions, learning about their professions and their activities, although he wasn't able to figure out how many of them fit within a strictly religious framework. There was, for example a botanist who spent his time classifying the rare species of the area; a geologist who was researching the ages and varieties of stones; other specialists who drew up maps or made graphs of the numbers of inhabitants in the area, their customs, their cultural level, the illnesses they were most susceptible to, and indexes of their deaths and births.

The technicians were efficient, well-paid people. In their wives you could often find the same unhappiness Liz felt, though occasionally one might amuse herself thinking about how she was going to astonish her friends in Iowa when she told them about her adventures in Ah-tún.

The American children attended school regularly, and in their free time they wandered around the outskirts of the camp. Their parents invariably forbid them from doing three things: drinking unpurified water, becoming friendly with strangers (especially if they were natives), and staying out after dark.

The second piece of advice, at least, was unnecessary. None of the children spoke any language other than English, which the *ladinos* in the area didn't know at all. Some Indians (the ones who worked in the houses in the camp, or who did manual labor for the technicians, or who attended the religious ceremonies with excessive regularity) had been able to learn a few words. But their timidity, their reserved nature, their ancestral respect for the *caxlanes* stopped them from saying those words except among themselves.

"As you can see," Pastor Williams finally explained to Arthur, "a linguist was indispensable for us. It's urgent that we begin to translate the Bible into Tzeltal. That's the only way we'll be able to preach effectively."

"We could print up leaflets too, and give them out free of charge, so that we can spread the Good Word even farther."

Pastor Williams smiled.

"That wouldn't do any good. The natives in this area are illiterate."

"Then why not open a school?"

"Take it easy, Smith, my friend. We can't do everything at once. When we decided to set ourselves up here, the most important thing was to clean up the area. They had everything here: malaria, parasitosis, typhoid fever. If we hadn't begun there, we would have been the first to die."

"And now?"

"We have to maintain our facilities. The water purifiers, the landing strips, the swimming pool."

"I've seen the Indians working there, and they don't get paid for it."

"Yes, that's their way of showing us their gratitude. But what's really expensive is the machinery, like the airplanes, for example, that always have to be ready."

At first Arthur had thought that only the helicopter was necessary. But now the hangars were full of four-engine planes.

"We had to build a camp," continued Pastor Williams, proudly. "When we came here, there was nothing but jungle. Now look at what we have. There's almost no reason for us to be homesick."

Almost. The only thing missing was a soda-fountain, or a bank branch.

"Well then," concluded Williams. "Your job at Ah-tún will be to do the translations we talked about. Take your time, my friend, we're in no hurry. And you won't have to do them in order. I'll tell you which verses will be read and discussed for each Sunday's meeting."

Arthur Smith was assigned an assistant: a young native man—Mariano Sántiz Nich—whose first-rank knowledge of English had never been challenged by anyone.

Arthur and Mariano worked together in a large room, at a comfortable table, with everything they needed for their work at hand. Mariano, docile as befit his station, sat facing the other man. But his greatest effort did not lie in concentrating on the texts, or in trying to penetrate their meaning, or in transferring them exactly from one language into another. The most difficult thing for him was to remain seated, to gaze at the trees and the countryside from a distance through a window pane, to use his hands in a task that did not demand ruggedness.

Mariano's face and neck would get drenched with sweat, and when Arthur asked him the precise meaning of a word, he would answer with the first thing that came into his head. And if the text said Holy Spirit, Mariano translated it as Sun, and virile element that fertilizes, and spade that turns the soil, and fingers that mold the clay. And if it said devil, he didn't think of evil, he wasn't afraid nor did he reject it. Instead he bowed his head in submission, because after all the devil was only the reverse side of that other power, and you had to make him conciliatory offerings and agree on useful alliances. What Mariano missed, because it was never mentioned, was the great birthing vagina that functions in darkness and never rests.

After several months Mariano was almost accustomed to this repose. But then Pastor Williams arranged for Arthur Smith and his assistant to begin the more active work of preaching in church.

Elderly people, nearly stone-like, came to the Sunday meetings: men hardened by weariness, women bent by the weight of their children. They looked around, secretly disappointed by the lack of ornamentation that was so abundant in the Catholic churches. But they awaited the sermon as such a supernatural event, that the first time Arthur Smith went up to the pulpit to speak to them he felt embarrassed.

Since it was his "debut", Pastor Williams had granted Arthur a free hand. And Arthur improvised a modest presentation of himself. He said that he had come from a far-away country, and that during his journey he had faced innumerable adversities and dangers. So then, what had moved him to set out on such a bold adventure? It was his zeal to spread the word of Christ, so that everyone, even those that the "world" in its frivolity and the "wise men" in their stupidity classify as the lowest, would have the opportunity to know the example of the great Teacher, to imitate Him and to find salvation. But, Arthur added humorously, this zeal of his was not without a selfish purpose. Here he remembered a phrase he had often heard from his mother's lips: "No one is saved alone. If you would find salvation, you must save another."

"So then, my brothers in Christ, you have nothing to thank me for. On the contrary, it is I who owe you a debt of gratitude. Because, thanks to the labor that I am undertaking with you, I hope to achieve what I so long for: the salvation of my soul."

The reactions among the American listeners were diverse, and immediately evident. Liz smiled with a tolerance that was very close to mockery. Pastor Williams said, though without much conviction,

"Well done, my son." The others pressed his hand with an automatic gesture that held a sense of uneasiness rather than congratulations.

Arthur would not admit to himself that he had failed until the respective specialists made known the results of their surveys among the native populace. No one had understood a word. And to make things worse, Mariano Sántiz Nich, who was supposed to know about these matters since he was Arthur's assistant, had been spreading the word (which if it wasn't subversive, was at least irreverent) that the "Christs" (as they called the Americans and whoever followed their doctrines) could not go to heaven and appear before their God unless they had an Indian by the hand, that this Indian was a sort of passport and they couldn't get in without him. And therefore they truly were the brothers, although the younger ones, of these other men, and were indispensable.

Pastor Williams did not become angry, but from that moment on he was unyielding in his demand that Arthur not stray from the pattern that he and his predecessors had established. Arthur obeyed.

There was very little that the people who attended the theological explanations understood clearly—whether they were blond or dark-skinned—especially when it came to the shades of difference between one Protestant sect and another, or when the Courtesan of Rome was condemned. But this served the Indians as an occasion to remember their own myths, to remove the crust that time, abandonment and oblivion had deposited on the faces of their ancient gods, making them unrecognizable.

When the time came to sing the psalms, the Indians felt that in that voice, trembling in some, out of tune in others, and off tempo in the rest, was the only moment during their week of hard struggle when something came out of them similar to wings, when a timeless knot became untied, when "the stone to the sepulchre was rolled away."

But the important thing, according to Pastor Williams, was to inculcate them with certain elementary morals. Initially, to extirpate the vices that were most deeply rooted in them, and the tenacity of this work had already produced its first fruits. He could now present his parishioners to any visitor without fear that one of them would do something to create a scandal. Because at first, many of them had come to the meetings intoxicated, and others saw nothing disrespectful about smoking in church.

Little by little (they are a good natured people, even if they do have limited intelligence, conceded the Pastor) they gave in to the rules that were always set forth in the name of Christ. In the name of Christ, many of them stopped drinking and smoking, to the point where this became the main feature distinguishing them from the Catholics in the area, who were always given over to drunkenness, fights and scandal.

The Pastor also tried to spread the most rudimentary practices of hygiene among his flock. Just what was necessary so that the crowds in church would not give off odors offensive to the pituitary glands of Americans, and so that neither they nor their household members would run the risk of carrying back home, hidden in the folds of their clothing, some horrible, infection-causing insect.

To this end they had installed some public baths near the church, and from time to time they gave out free packages of hair oil scented with DDT.

Every day the Organization won over new members. Soon, Pastor Williams assured them, they would have to enlarge the camp, put up more buildings for prayer, find new collaborators for their work.

Arthur Smith awaited the praise that he expected for the small grain of sand he was contributing toward this success. The translations from the Bible to Tzeltal were precisely the catalyzing element that had been missing up until then. That praise never came. Arthur Smith was to be glad about that later on, when the problems began to arise.

The first was with the Indian Aid Mission. Despite the fact that the Organization had lent them assistance in difficult times (transporting seriously ill or distinguished persons by helicopter, loaning out vaccines whenever there was the danger of an epidemic), the Mission objected to some of the theoretical points that served as the basis for the Organization's work.

In the first place, they didn't bother to teach the Indians Spanish. When one of them emerged from monolingualism, it was to express himself in a language foreign to the nation's culture: English. Furthermore, they gave no thought to the teaching of civics. The Organization never uttered the word Mexico in front of the Indians, and if they did, it was not to explain that they, the Indians, were citizens of the country of that name and therefore were entitled to demand certain rights from the Government, but also had to meet certain obligations required of them.

As for their educational approach, the Organization's way of handling it was not only contrary, but contradictory to the official one, based on Article Three of the Mexican Constitution. The Organization gave a religious explanation for the origin of the world and its phenomena, and upheld its assertions with books it considered to be dictated directly by God. Article Three stood for secular teaching, and maintained that man's reason was the only appropriate guide to the labyrinth of facts confronting him, the only thing capable of establishing laws of cause and effect (apart, of course, from miracles) and of finding norms of conduct that would ennoble and strengthen human dignity.

These discrepancies gave rise to an enormous exchange of correspondence. The Mission took its protest to the State Government, but got nothing in return except the traditional washing of Pilate's hands, and a promise to refer the matter to the higher authority of the Government of the Republic. From that office the Mission received an official letter, calling freedom of religion "one of the most treasured achievements of our Revolutions," and asserting that the Organization was fulfilling all the necessary requirements and all its documents were in order to operate in that region just as it was doing. The letter ended with a call for harmony and cooperation. Why was it necessary for two organisms that were pursuing common goals—although by different means—to become rivals and to block one another? The Indian problem was so vast and complex that it could be solved only with the participation of everyone, both official and private institutions, no matter what their nationality or ideology.

The Mission had to accept this and put the best possible face on things. But the priest in Oxchuc, who defended interests that were much more immediate and concrete, went on the attack. He and the Organization shared the same territory. If they could brandish a newly imported Christ, he could count on the centuries of tradition of his church, in which it was not necessary to pronounce any name, explain any doctrine, or uncover any mystery. For him to prosper, personally, it had been enough merely to make an annual trek through his parish, performing certain ceremonies at which the Indian population gathered en masse: baptisms, extreme unctions, marriages. These ceremonies, which in Indian eyes always held a sense of magic (they drove off evil powers, made the rains fall at the proper time, caused the crops to grow in abundance) were paid for generously. The priest returned to Ciudad Real to enjoy his earnings for months.

But those earnings had been diminishing lately. First, the village of Ah-tún, an insignificant place, stopped giving tithes and offerings to the parish. That was tolerable, it could be explained by the presence of the gringos. But the gringos weren't going to go out to the Tzeltal region. They have a reputation for liking their creature comforts, they aren't capable of surviving for long so far from civilization.

The priest of Oxchuc soon stopped fooling himself. He discovered that the gringos didn't deprive themselves of a thing, and that every helicopter flight brought in new parts to complete their equipment, and new people to add to their personnel.

Evidently, the Organization planned to set up a permanent establishment in Ah-tún. So the priest from Oxchuc appealed to the Bishop of Chiapas, who was located in Ciudad Real.

There, an urgent conclave of urban and rural priests was called and long deliberations held. The result of this was the recognition by Catholic clergymen that they had been negligent in caring for their flock. The wolf had taken advantage of the situation in order to enter the fold and devour the sheep at its ease. Their error had to be corrected immediately.

An intense campaign was undertaken, embracing the entire municipality of Oxchuc. Others, many others, joined the parish priest to begin visiting small villages, isolated areas. It was a sacrifice because they had only the most primitive, uncomfortable means of transportation at their disposal.

From the pulpits, the priests thundered against the discord that was spreading out from Ah-tún. They told the history of previous schisms. They unmasked the secret vices of Luther and Calvin, they exposed the lechery of Henry VIII, they condemned the skepticism of the French monarchs. The Indians listened, dumbfounded. But the priests always ended up going back to something very near at hand, that anyone could sense from his own experience: the Tzeltales were divided. There were some, the Christs, who neither smoked nor drank so that they could feel superior to the others, who, more humble and more faithful, zealously guarded the traditions of their fathers and their grandfathers.

The only thing that could come out of this situation, went on the implacable syllogism of the priests, were terrible evils. The punishment of God, my children. The bolt of lightning that strikes the traveler, the fever that consumes little babies, the hunger that cannot be satisfied because there is no corn, the *brujo* whose evil doings no man has the power to undo. And in the dark of night, the *Negro Cimarrón* stealing away young maidens; the *Yehualcihautl* luring men to perdition and death; the skeleton of the adulterous woman, whose bones clank together lugubriously, like a warning of misfortune.

The Indians came out of the church overwhelmed with anguish and rage. They went straight to the town's liquor stores and quickly drank themselves into a state of intoxication. On the way back to their huts they took out their machetes and hacked through the air with clumsy, ferocious blows that split the defenseless trunk of some tree.

The Christs tried to avoid any ugly, dangerous encounters. They spent Sunday, a holy day, in church, singing and praying in turn, and in the evening they went back to their villages along seldom-traveled paths and even over improvised roads.

They did not inform Pastor Williams of their uneasiness or their fears. And the meteorologists at the camp of Ah-tún, so attentive to the slightest change in the atmosphere and so meticulous at noting them down, did not notice that a storm-cloud was forming all around them.

Meanwhile, everything went along with its usual rhythm. Mariano Sántiz Nich continued to show up punctually for work. He only missed the day his eldest son died. But the following day he was there again, sitting erect in his chair, ready to carry out his superior's order.

Arthur did not know where to begin. He had to mention Mariano's loss in some way. Surely, among Indians there had to exist formulaic phrases to express feelings at times like these. But Arthur didn't know them, and he was afraid of being tactless if he used his own phrases. But there was something else, besides this, that disturbed him. What did it mean to Mariano that his child had died? Judging from his attitude, it wasn't important at all.

"How old was he?" Arthur finally asked.

"He was going on twelve."

(Then, this man must have become a father at almost that same age. And his wife is even younger than he is. Marriages at such an early age should be outlawed, thought Arthur.)

"And what did he die of?"

It was like digging into a wound. But apparently there was no wound.

"Of a fever."

"But what did the doctor say?"

"That the sickness was called typhoid."

"Don't they boil the drinking water at your house?"

"No."

"Hasn't anyone ever told you that the water you drink is full of microbes, and it's the microbes that cause that sickness?"

Mariano made an ambiguous gesture. His indifference exasperated Arthur.

"If they had boiled the water, your son would be alive today."

He didn't say these things out of cruelty. Mariano had other children; they were in danger of dying too.

Arthur's assistant didn't seem very affected or convinced by the argument.

"My oldest son is in heaven. There is no hunger there, no cold, no beatings. He's happy there."

And he bent over the notebook in front of him, ready to begin writing.

That evening, Arthur Smith went looking for Pastor Williams to discuss this episode that had disturbed him so much. But he found the house dark, and in spite of the fact that he stayed there knocking for more than a quarter of an hour, no one answered. A neighbor finally stuck his head out the window to tell him that Liz had left to spend a few months in the United States on vacation. The children had gone with her, and the Pastor most probably would be taking advantage of their absence.

No one knew exactly the way Pastor Williams took advantage of his family's absences, but everyone denounced it energetically. Some guessed that he frequented the brothels in Tuxtla or Ciudad Real; others thought he kept a mistress in Oxchuc, a slovenly old mestiza; and finally, there were some who thought he made pastoral visits to the natives' huts when the men were out in the maize fields.

Arthur refused to give credence to this gossip. After all, where did it come from? From wicked, idle women who spent the entire day painting their nails, filling their heads with nothing but the filth of the "confidential stories", the "true romances", and the mixtures of sex and violence that they received greedily every week, thanks to the helicopter.

As for the men... Some of them were passible. The botanist, for example. He was always absorbed with the nervature of a leaf, or making unimaginable calculations to determine how young or old a plant was. Human beings, including in this genre his wife, didn't interest him. He was nice to everyone because that made everything go easier for him, and it avoided conflicts that would have required more attention later on. He could differentiate the natives from his compatriots by their odor (old, yellowed wool, or what else was it?), and since he didn't like the smell, he tried to keep his distance from them. As far as everything else was concerned, the only thing he needed for his work was the occasional assistance of a guide.

The geologist was something else entirely. He suffered from a roving fanaticism whose only constant lay in the ferocity of its expression. Sometimes the object of his exalted state was his country's power, to whose enrichment and preservation he was currently contributing in some obscure, anonymous, but effective way. But if necessary, he swore, he was ready to defend it, even at the cost of however many lives were at his disposal.

At other times he raised up his exterminating bolt against heretics in both the religious and the political fields, and even in that of sports. Purity, perfection and infallibility, which he served as a nucleus, had to be preserved against any sort of contamination. And at incoherent intervals, the geologist would condemn those that he considered the carriers of contagious germs. Right now Pastor Williams was playing that role. During his escapes, he had fallen into ignominious circumstances even worse than those of the helicopter pilot or the radio technician. Aside from the fact that they would be more useful to the Nation in a time of danger, the only thing they did was look at photographs of naked women. And of American women at that. But this other man...

What they needed at the Ah-tún camp, concluded the geologist, was to create a Commission for the Purification of Honor and Justice. Its function would be to hold monthly meetings where each and every person's orthodoxy could be examined publicly, to reward those who deserved it and to ensure that anyone who had committed some serious error would not go unpunished. How many things would be brought to light! What surprises they would all be in for!

"Wouldn't that be a little indiscreet?" Arthur ventured to suggest.

No, rebutted the geologist vigorously. It would put into practice the true spirit of American democracy. A spirit that, far from home, was in danger of corruption.

Arthur did not contradict these statements, because of an instinctive fear that his own orthodoxy would be the first to be suspected. Cordially, he left the geologist. But all these precautions were not sufficient. The suspicious gaze of his questioner followed him, like a bird of prey, all the way down the street.

Since Williams still hadn't come back, Arthur went to talk to the doctor. He wanted him to explain the death of Mariano's son, to justify it if he could.

Arthur had to go into detail before the doctor knew who he was talking about. Oh, yes! He had gone to see him at the very end, and by that time nothing could be done. The natives never think anything is serious until it's already hopeless.

"But typhoid is curable, doctor. There are antibiotics..."

At any rate they would have been useless in this case. Even had they been used in time. The boy had reached such an extreme point of malnutrition that he couldn't have survived even a cold.

"Couldn't measures be taken to make sure things like this won't happen again?" insisted Arthur. "The Organization could send food, and we could give it out."

"The Organization has a special office for nutritional matters. Many factories donate their excess products, and an arrangement has been set up in the United States with the railroad companies to ship that sort of cargo without cost. We could fill the storerooms in the Ah-tún camp to the ceiling with cans of powdered milk, boxes of cereal, and all sorts of other packaged foods."

"Then why don't you?"

"We tried to once. Everything went fine until the shipment reached the border at the Rio Grande. And there it stopped. The Mexican trains were demanding a freight fee, and their tariffs are extremely high."

"But the Organization has plenty of money to pay them!"

"Of course it does. But it was a matter of principle. When it comes to charity, the country that receives the benefit, Mexico in this case, should collaborate. Now the Organization sends food only to those countries where we own the railroads."

"So then there's nothing we can do about it."

"Now don't go and judge work that's as important as this by one isolated case. The figures are all here: take a good look and compare them. One child dies, but so many others are saved. We have penicillin, sulfides, tonics..."

"Yes, their lives are saved to go on suffering from hunger, cold, beatings. I think Mariano was right after all."

"What are you talking about?" asked the doctor.

"Nothing, Doctor. Don't pay any attention to me. I'm a little shaky. I haven't been able to sleep for several nights in a row."

"Wait a moment. I'll give you a sedative."

It was a small bottle filled with red pills.

"Take just one, before you go to bed. And only when you think you absolutely need to."

That night Arthur Smith slept as he hadn't slept since he was a baby: quietly, deeply, without dreaming, without those furtive images that he pursued without ever being able to catch them. He woke up with a slightly vague sensation that he had been on the verge of discovering something important, very important. But this fogginess was quickly replaced by the strong certainty that everything was in order.

Arthur sang (how long had it been since he had done that?) while he was in the shower; he breakfasted heartily, and feeling fresh, energetic, euphoric, he got down to work.

Mariano sat, facing him, but his presence didn't give rise to any troublesome thought. Death —of loved ones, of oneself— the link that had bound them together for a moment the previous day was broken. Now, a table full of papers that one knew well and the other didn't understand was spread between them once more.

Shortly after eleven o'clock an Indian messenger arrived to notify Arthur that Pastor Williams had returned and was waiting for him in his study.

"Is there some problem?" he asked by way of greeting. "I hear that you've been roaming around the camp like a dog without his master."

"Well, actually," answered Arthur, "I don't quite know how to put it. Something painful has happened."

(Painful? Arthur didn't feel the slightest bit of pain anymore.)

"The death of Mariano's son?"

"How did you know?"

"I was there, right up to the end. Consoling them, as is my duty."

Arthur hesitated before he went on.

"Well, then, I don't know why, but suddenly the idea came into my head that this death could have been avoided."

"Remember, it is written: 'Not a leaf stirs but that it is the will of the Lord.'"

"Yes, but we have an obligation to put all our effort into saving what is worthy. And the life of a child, even an Indian child, is worth a lot."

"Are you insinuating that the doctor was negligent?"

"No, he already explained to me that Mariano's son was very weak, and that he had hardly any resistance left. He also explained to me that it's impossible for the Organization to send food to Mexico. But couldn't we try something else?"

"Do you have a suggestion?"

"Well, to begin with, the botanist could try out some new farming methods, manure, fertilizers. The Indians would eat better."

"The botanist has a very concrete and useful job to do."

"I don't doubt that. Some day, in the distant future, it may be useful. But in the meantime we have a child here who has died of hunger!"

"Besides," continued the Pastor, as if he hadn't heard Arthur's last sentence, although that was the one he had emphasized most, "you're confusing specialists. A botanist is not an agricultural engineer."

"Then, why not replace him with an agricultural engineer? Since the Organization has the luxury of paying for so many employees, at least let it choose the ones that are most urgently needed."

"You know that the Organization isn't autonomous. And the criteria for deciding who is most needed and who is needed less at the Ah-tún camp aren't only it's own, but also those of the United States Government."

This revelation momentarily stunned Arthur.

"Now I see why the geologist, the radio technician and the others are here. I never could figure out how they were contributing to the spreading of the teachings of Christ."

There was a pause. A short one. Arthur insisted.

"Tell me then, what the devil are those men doing here?"

Pastor Williams looked at Arthur with something worse that harshness: pity.

"Protecting us."

"From whom? From those poor Indians who come to sing psalms in church?"

"With the natives, you never know how they're going to react, or what they're scheming up in those primitive, savage minds of theirs. And those poor Indians, as you call them, aren't the only ones. There are others, and they're the great majority: the Catholics, whose priests are trying to get them to go after us."

Pastor Williams observed the surprise on Arthur's face with satisfaction.

"Would you like a cigarette?"

"I think I need one."

Williams held out the open box.

"And what if violence breaks out?"

"They wouldn't dare to attack the camp. They're well aware that we've got airplanes and weapons."

"Even so I don't like this whole idea. Christ preached peace."

"But he also said, 'I come not to bring peace, but a sword.' And you just said yourself that when we want to accomplish something worthwhile, we have to fight for it."

Arthur took a final drag on his cigarette, then smashed the butt out in an ashtray.

"Why are we fighting, Pastor?"

For a moment Williams didn't know what to answer.

"It's so obvious. . ."

"Yes, it's obvious that we Americans have a whole birthright of ideals, traditions, wealth and interests to preserve, to defend, and if possible to increase. But the Indians, what do they have? They've lost all their links with the past, and their present is overwhelmingly oppressive. And then we come along, with our air of benefactors, to give them... what?"

"I'll take the very case that has brought up this problem. You saw Mariano after his son died, didn't you?"

"Yes."

"Did he look desperate, sad, or even unresigned to you?"

"No."

"Well, he owes that to us. We've given him something he didn't have before: hope in the future."

"Hope is enough for the natives, as you call them, isn't it? But it's not enough for an American citizen. Not you, not anyone like you, not even I would be satisfied with the promise of a banquet that was going to be held at a place and on a date that hadn't been set. We all demand our share of meat, and enough bread to eat. And we want it today."

"I don't understand what it is you're driving at."

"Neither do I. Excuse me, Pastor. I've taken up too much of your time."

"If you're feeling disturbed or not well..."

"The doctor and I already talked about that. It turns out that, just like the Indians, I don't need medicine. What I need are sedatives."

Sedatives. Arthur Smith was glad that it was finally time to take them. Oh, how he needed to sleep, suddenly, completely, like a stone, like the trunk of a tree!

Because while he was still awake, after he had finished his work day, Arthur Smith didn't know what to do with his time. Since he was a bachelor (who could have taken the place of his mother?), the wives of all the other men regarded him with misgivings, and wouldn't let their husbands invite him to their homes. The only one who sometimes rebelled against this tacit agreement was the radio technician, who liked to play poker and couldn't always find other players.

"So, what are the Catholic Indians up to? Are they still causing trouble?" Arthur Smith asked him.

The radio technician shuffled the cards with the dexterity of a cardsharp.

"That's all crap! They wouldn't dare try anything serious."

"Then you people, I mean the ones here to protect us, you must be getting bored with nothing to do."

"Things aren't always this quiet. We have to be on guard all the time. Once in a while we make a fat catch, and then we earn our keep. That's for sure!"

"A fat catch?" repeated Arthur, uncomprehending.

"We have a whole file of photographs, of physical descriptions. Some of them even go as far as having plastic surgery to avoid being recognized. Like the John Perkins case — remember him? He thought he could shake us. Every police force in the United States had been after him for months. He was able to fool them all, and he even got as far as the Guatemalan border. That's where we finally caught up with him."

"What crime had he committed?"

The radio technician dealt the cards.

"Espionage."

The game was going to be a challenge. But Arthur Smith couldn't concentrate on it.

"Did he go on trial?"

"Who? Perkins? Sure. The trial was sensational. Headlines in all the newspapers. There was a lot of controversy about the whole thing because they found him guilty on circumstantial evidence. And Perkins swore he was innocent right up to the moment they strapped him into the electric chair."

A wave of nausea suddenly swept over Arthur Smith.

"What's wrong with you?" asked the radio-technician brusquely. "You're looking pale. Do you want some whiskey?"

"No, don't bother," answered Arthur, standing up. "I think I just need some fresh air."

That guy doesn't have any guts at all, decided the radio technician as he watched him go.

Arthur walked off from the only road in the camp and got as far as the river bank. In that solitude he could contemplate the shining stars in all their purity. But something in his eyes —something tremulous, irritating—stopped him from making them out very well.

When it was time for bed, Arthur decided not to take the barbiturates.

"What do I have to be afraid of? As Pastor Williams says, we're being protected. The watchdogs are looking out for us. They have a good nose, and sharp teeth. The radio technician just showed me his."

Suddenly Arthur Smith noticed that he was sweating. And his sweat was cold, the way it is when anguish or terror become intolerable.

"It's not my enemy I'm afraid of: it's my protector."

Automatically his hand reached for the bottle of red pills. When he realized that he had only one pill left, and that it wouldn't be enough since he had been taking higher dosages, he quickly put his clothes back on and went to wake up the doctor. He had to make up a lie: the bottle had broken, and the pills had gone down the drain.

"You should try to stop taking them. Addiction is very harmful."

"Don't worry about me, doctor, I'm well protected."

Like a prisoner in jail is. That was Arthur's last conscious thought. A minute later he was snoring.

Waking up wasn't as pleasant for Arthur now as it had been before. He had an upset stomach, there was a buzzing noise echoing in his head, and he found it difficult to keep his thoughts straight or talk in coherent sentences. But all these inconveniences had one consolation: the indifference he could feel towards everything happening around him.

Everyone else, however, seemed very excited. Liz had written to the Pastor, telling him that she was filing for divorce on grounds of mental cruelty, and the people in the camp were placing bets on the sort of attitude Williams would take. Would he bring his mistress from Oxchuc to live with him in his own house? That would be an insult that no one would tolerate. Would he publicly recognize the son he had had by a native woman? The relationship was not an hypothesis of evil minds, but a fact that the physical resemblance made undeniable. Would he ask for a leave to take a trip to the United States, and try to seek a reconciliation with his wife?

Far away from these speculations, Pastor Williams was clearly worried about another kind of problem: the Catholics had really begun to go over the line. Their latest ugly act had been to go looking for one of the Christs out in his maize field, and to threaten to kill him if he didn't finish off a bottle of whiskey right then and there and smoke every single cigarette they gave him. The Christ had given in to their threats, but two days later, after the effects of the drunk and his intoxication from tobacco had worn off, he went to the church in Ah-tún to publicly confess his cowardice—he should have died like a martyr!—declare himself unworthy of belonging to a community of chosen people, and ask forgiveness for his sins.

Pastor Williams asked the gathering of the faithful to show benevolence. But the natives turned their backs on the penitent, and more than one, walking past, spat on him. The condemned man did not raise his head. He left the church, his village, and his family, and went to the place where men die, on the coast.

On one of the following days, Arthur asked Mariano (without enthusiasm, because he really wasn't interested in the answer) what he would have done if he had been the apostate. Mariano said that he didn't want to sin, that he didn't want to go to hell. That when he died, he would be with his oldest child, in heaven, and there, no one would be able to separate them.

This was, perhaps, the only allusion made to an incident that the Americans decided was unimportant and of no consequence.

But the Indians have a capricious memory. They forget favors (they receive so few, and pay dearly in so many ways!) while an offence against them becomes a fixed idea from which they can only be freed through vengeance.

And those same Christs who had thrown the apostate out of the church like a mangy sheep were the ones who by night, stealthily and relentlessly, set fire to the Catholic village of Bumiljá.

Retaliation came immediately. Christs murdered at the crossroads, huts plundered, crops burned.

From the high altar of the church at Oxchuc the priest gave his blessing.

The news reached the camp at Ah-tún distorted by hate and alarm, and when it did, it was blown out of proportion to the point of disbelief, owing to the need that isolated groups have to break the tedium of their unchanging days with some extraordinary event.

Pastor Williams called his collaborators to a general assembly in the meeting hall. His purpose was to discuss the most prudent way of responding to the emergency at hand.

The geologist proposed immediate action. Weren't the airplanes just getting rusty in the hangars? Didn't they have a full arsenal of weapons? All right then, the time had come to use them. A small, clean, effective bombing of Oxchuc and its surroundings, and the Catholics would learn their lesson.

Arthur Smith stood up, livid with rage, stammering. That would be, he said, a crime against defenseless people —women, children, old people— not involved in what was going on. It was others who were really responsible, he finished. And he sat back down, breathless, wiping the perspiration from his face with a handkerchief.

Pastor Williams made a joking remark about Arthur's vehemence, and added that he was against the geologist's suggestion too, but for different reasons. In his far-off youth (quiet murmurs of protest were heard here) he had studied the basic notions of international law. An attack like the one the geologist had proposed constituted, of course, the violation of a foreign territory. They could only resort to such measures in extreme cases, when American citizens' lives or property were endangered. But that was not the present situation, and to be unduly harsh would only have the effect of damaging the highly cordial relationship that existed between the United States and Mexico. In the long run, it could even lead to the cancellation of the Organization's permission to install one of its dependent groups in Ah-tún. And that would not be productive.

No, Pastor Williams' plan was much more simple, more direct, and perhaps for that very reason, more effective: they would meet with the people who were really responsible, the ones Arthur had alluded to, probably without knowing their names or their ecclesiastical titles. They were Manuel Oropeza, the Bishop of Chiapas; Teodoro Hernández, the priest in Oxchuc, and others of lesser importance.

Pastor Williams' opinion prevailed over the others, not because it was more reasonable, but because the Pastor had recovered his prestige and his moral authority since his conduct as a divorced man had remained impeccable. All those rumors (that he frequented brothels, that he cohabited with mestizas, that he had secretly fathered children) boiled down to nothing, lacking a foundation. The Pastor, always easily located, always with witnesses or an explanation for his every act, appeared discreetly sad at appropriate times, generously disposed to assume blame when necessary and with the sportsmanlike desire that Liz would find a suitable husband and lasting happiness.

When the assembly applauded his motion, it was also applauding a man who had shown his integrity at a difficult moment, his fortitude in overcoming adversity, and an indomitable, optimistic spirit.

While Pastor Williams was in Ciudad Real, conferring with the Bishop and his allies, some isolated acts of violence were still taking place in the Municipality of Oxchuc. Among them was the death of Mariano Sántiz Nich, hacked down with a machete.

When Arthur heard the news, the callousness with which he accepted it surprised him. In the end, despite the work they had engaged in together for so many months, they had never been anything but strangers to each other.

But that night Arthur had to take a triple dose of barbiturates.

He was hoping that he would wake up with dulled senses, and yet from the very first moment a strange, painful lucidity assaulted him. He suddenly realized that he could reconstruct, trace by trace, the features of the man who had been his assistant. And that in spite of the fact that he had never noticed it then, now he could remember the man's peculiar way of holding the pencil he used to write; of running his fingers through his hair when the effort to pay attention was too much; of smiling, as if to himself, when he had understood something.

Arthur realized, finally, that the one who had died was not a number on a list of statistics, not a native with exotic customs and dress, not a thing you could mold with a very sophisticated propaganda machine. The one who had died was a man with doubts, like Arthur; with fears like him, with useless moments of rebellion, with memories, with irreparable losses, with a hope that was stronger than common sense.

And in this sense of solidarity that Arthur had suddenly discovered, there was still one more element. He matched his mother's words ("no one is saved alone") with their complement, added by Mariano after his first sermon.

"He was the one who could have saved me, if I had been able to save him. Mariano would have opened the gates of heaven for me, and we would have walked in together, hand in hand."

This idea suddenly brought him a feeling of intolerable desperation. He tried to put it out of his mind.

"This is madness. I'm losing control of myself."

Upset, he went to the doctor's office. He needed a stronger sedative, he said. The one he had prescribed didn't work any more.

"It would be against my professional ethics if I gave you a medication that clearly is hurting you. Your recent faults in behavior could be blamed on the abuse of barbiturates. Because otherwise..."

Arthur, irritated by the doctor's refusal, asked defiantly:

"Otherwise, what?"

"We would have to judge you in a harsher light."

"Judges everywhere, accusers, executioners!"

And Arthur walked out of the office, slamming the door behind him.

Pastor Williams returned in triumph. In the report he presented to the assembly, he said that he had found a spirit of conciliation among all the clergy of Chiapas, especially the Bishop (an accessible, likeable man who understood every aspect of the situation). He said that after several very cordial conversations, they had established very clearly what their respective zones of influence would be, and both sides had made a commitment to respect this with the utmost scrupulousness, so that in the future any possible discord could be avoided.

"To sum it all up," ended the Pastor, "things will once again be running smoothly."

"What about the blood that's already been spilled?"

It was Arthur Smith, of course. And he was crying out not for some anonymous, impersonal blood, but for the blood of men just like him, just like all the others; men who, if they had been given the chance, a little time, would have become their friends, their brothers. He was crying out for Mariano's blood.

Some booed the interruption. But the Pastor imposed silence with a gesture that demanded both obedience to his authority and compassion for the misguided lamb.

"That blood which, after all, we can't recover, has not been spilled in vain. One of the Bishop's relatives, a priest who has vast experience with the natives of Chiapas, was kind enough to explain to me that it is useful to have a blood-letting from time to time, the way it was in the Middle Ages when they bled people who were suffering from congestion. You see, when the Indians attack each other, they're finding an escape valve for that irrational, blind, demoniacal hatred that poisons their souls and that, if it didn't find that release, would explode in an uprising against the whites."

"So then, Pastor Williams, this trip to Ciudad Real has led you to discover that racial solidarity exists between the Courtesan of Rome and the Brothers of Christ."

Arthur Smith again. Couldn't he just shut up?

"Not only racial. Remember our common origin, the traditions we share. Any theological discrepancy, any historical separation is beside the point when all Christians are faced with a common enemy."

"Who is that? The devil?"

The radio-technician broke in noisily. Was it possible that Arthur Smith wasn't aware of what was happening in the world? Well, if Arthur wanted to fill himself in, he personally was ready to put at his disposal an instrument on which every day, at the same time, he could hear the news bulletin transmitted from America.

"The devil, if that's what you want to call it," continued Pastor Williams, as if the interruption had never taken place. "But most people know it by the name of Communism."

Arthur burst out laughing.

"And would you mind telling me where there are any Communists around here? The only thing I've seen, in all the Tzeltal region I've been in, is misery, ignorance, superstition, filth, fanaticism. Is that the way Communists reveal or hide themselves?"

"I told you once about how the spy, John Perkins, was captured," said the radio-technician.

"Oh, yes. I forgot to congratulate you on your glorious achievement. Thanks to you, they fried him in the electric chair."

"I won't allow myself to be insulted by a traitor!"

There was an uproar in the hall. Someone held back the radio-technician; others, with seeming repugnance, stopped Arthur. Nobody was paying any attention to the geologist, who punched Arthur Smith right in the face.

Pastor Williams shouted with a loud, authoritative voice:

"Gentlemen, the meeting is adjourned!"

While everyone else left in small groups of friends, of conspirators, of men who only knew how to latch on to others, Arthur Smith went back alone to his solitary room in the guest house.

He turned on the bathroom light and looked at himself in the medicine-chest mirror.

"What a punch. That guy obviously knew what he was doing."

He applied several hot compresses to the painful area, and got ready for bed.

"I'm not going to be able to sleep," he thought.

But it was strange. That certainty, which would have upset him at other times, didn't even bother him today. And his fear (how? why?) had vanished.

"I have all night, the whole night long, and maybe the rest of my life to think. I need to think a lot; I need to be able to understand what's happening."

Because now everything that had previously been so neat and marked clearly with a label had become confusing and incomprehensible. There were no definite lines between the good side and the bad side; the villain and the hero were no longer two adversaries confronting each other, but a single face with two masks. Victory was no longer a reward won by the good, but booty taken by the cunning, by the strong.

The following day Arthur Smith appeared in Williams' office. The latter didn't make even the slightest gesture of welcome.

"I suppose you're handing in your resignation."

"Yes. But not under the terms you think. First, I demand that you give me some answer about the fraud you've perpetrated on me."

"Fraud? Are you crazy?"

"In the United States, in the offices of the Organization, I was told that in the House of the Lord there are many mansions, and that Ah-tún was one of them. And then it turns out that there's nothing but a flimsy facade full of cracks, and hidden behind them are..."

"That's enough!"

"Yes, it is enough. I don't need to name what you know better than I do, since you're covering it up."

"God and Country always go together. I don't have anything to be ashamed of. And in a time of struggle..."

"Why bring the struggle to this place?"

"Because there's not a single place in the world that hasn't been turned into a battleground. Because Latin America is part of our Hemisphere. And because Communism is infiltrating Latin America more each day."

"It's strange. Communism infiltrates countries where few have the right to eat or to get an education. Where dignity is a luxury that only the rich can afford, and humiliation is a part of being poor. Where a handful of men with dignity, well-educated and well-fed, exploit the humbled, ignorant, hungry masses."

"Have you finished your sermon?"

"It wasn't a sermon. Didn't you notice that I didn't mention any of the great words? Not love, gentleness or forgiveness. Those are the words we use to dress up our Sundays. I was asking for what should be our daily bread: justice."

Pastor Williams lit up a cigarette, insolently.

"My advice to you is to stay as far away from it as you can."

"You thought I meant 'police' when I said 'justice'. The one who should keep his distance from that is you."

Pastor Williams ground his cigarette into the ashtray.

"As for your departure from the Ah-tún camp, you should make it as soon as possible. And as for the means you may have counted on to do so, I should advise you that the helicopter is not among them."

"Thank you. I guessed as much."

"And I should warn you too that I've sent a complete report to my superiors in the Organization about your personality, your conduct in Ah-tún, and your recent activities. At first I chalked them up to emotional outbursts, but now I see they were part of a deliberate, dire intention."

"I admire your perspicacity, Pastor."

"Don't try to be clever. That report of mine will be distributed in the appropriate places. It will make life impossible for you in America. You won't be able to find work because nobody wants to hire a traitor. You won't have any friends because everyone avoids a person who's suspect, like they would the plague."

"And they wouldn't let me go to jail?"

"Not even that."

"Is that because they don't have enough evidence to accuse me?"

"It's because you aren't important enough. The State won't support a bum."

"Sometimes you're very persuasive, Pastor. But I'm not going back to the Unites States. Not for now, at least."

"Do you intend to stay here? You should know that we won't allow you to live in the areas that are under our control, and neither will the Catholics."

"But there are other areas. Good-bye, Pastor."

Arthur Smith did not put out his hand to shake the other man's goodbye. He simply left. He went to his room to pack his things, only the indispensable items, because from now on he would have to carry them himself.

He picked up a copy of the Gospels, worn with use. It was a gift from his mother, and it had been his favorite book since childhood. He loved it. But now the others had vilified it. He let it go.

"I don't want them to think that I'm like the all the rest."

When Arthur walked down the sole, long, straight street of Ah-tún, no one looked out at him. It was time for the radio serial. Only the Pastor, behind his window, murmured to himself.

"That stupid imbecile. He could have had a fine career."

Arthur walked in the fresh, aromatic, shifting shade of the pine trees. Then over a small plain. At dusk he sat down to rest against a rock.

How beautiful the countryside was! And how free he felt, because not one thing that he contemplated made him feel greedy, nothing awakened a possessive instinct in him!

"So then, Arthur," he said finally to himself. "It's time to do some reckoning. Here you are, out in the cold. Overnight, you've lost all the props that were supporting you. Now there's no more religion, or country, or money."

He breathed calmly. He didn't feel nostalgia, or fear, or a sense of abandonment. Just like Mariano, the only thing he had was hope.

"I'm young. And the only thing I need is time. Time to understand, to decide."

Far off, in the sunset, smoke arose from a hut, the slight, hesitant smoke of a poor kitchen. Arthur began walking toward it.

"I'm hungry. Maybe they'll let me stay there for one night. There must be something useful I can do for them."

Arthur walked quickly, anxious to get there.

"We'll just have to come to an agreement. At least these men and I speak the same language."

GLOSSARY

***aceite guapo*:** whiskey, so bad that it can kill the person who drinks it.

acitrones: cactus candy.

africanos: See *tartaritas*.

ajwalil: boss.

bolom: a general term for wild felines such as the jaguar. They are companion spirits of strong, fat, handsome people. If one is heard roaring, its name is not to be uttered, as that might provoke it to attack.

brujo: a conjurer. a male witch.

cachuco: a silver coin struck under the direction of Carrasco during the Revolution.

Castilla: term used by the Indians to denote the Spanish language.

caxlán: from the Spanish word, Castilian. A white man, or a half-caste or Indian who dresses like a townsman and can read and write Spanish. Cunning, crafty. Also called a *ladino*.

chamulas: Indians from Chiapas who are part of an ancient aboriginal tribe that still survives today. *Chamulita*: the diminutive of the word; disdainful in tone.

chepe loco: a child's game. Literally, *chepe* is the diminutive of José or Josefa; *loco* means mad or insane.

chimbos: candy made with eggs, almonds and syrup.

chulel: every person's protective spirit.

Ciudad Real: located in the highlands of the south of Mexico, this town was established in 1528 as a settlement by the Spanish conquerors. In 1536 it was incorporated as a city and for a time was the capital of the state of Chiapas. In 1823 its name was changed to San Cristóbal de las Casas in honor of the Dominican preacher, Bartolomé de las Casas, champion of the rights of Indians, who had been a bishop in the diocese. The indigenous name for this site is Jobel.

coletos **(m);** ***coletas*** **(f)**: a disdainful term given to the residents of the state of Chiapas, and particularly to the inhabitants of the city of San Cristóbal las Casas.

diezmo: tithes.

encomenderos: in the New World, *encomiendas* or land grants were established by the conquering Spaniards. The Indians lived on these and worked permanently for an *encomendero* or "protector", much as the serfs in medieval times had worked for a feudal lord.

escopeta: rifle.

Jobel: See Ciudad Real.

ladino: See *caxlán*.

macho **bananas**: a large banana grown in Mexico.

martoma: custodian of the image of a saint. (Spanish: *mayordomo*.)

nahual: a sorcerer (*brujo*) that changes shape by means of enchantment.

posh: whiskey made of sugar cane.

posol: corn meal dissolved in water and used as a drink by the natives.

pukuj: devil, witch, demon.

reales: coins used in Mexico until recently.

takín: money.

tartaritas, africanos: names of candy, but they also refer to countries (Tatary, Africa), and are therefore more exotic.

tatik: father.

tayacanes: guides

tostones: coins of silver, worth about four *reales*.

Tzeltal: a dialect derived from Maya. One of the indigenous languages spoken in Chiapas.

Tzotziles: Indian tribes of Central America: inhabitants of Guatemala, Yucatán, and the state of Chiapas in Mexico. Also the name of the language: *Tzotzil*.

ventana: window.

Villafuerte: ***fuerte*** = strong; ***villa*** = town.

waigel: the protective spirit of the tribe. A feline animal: tiger or jaguar.

yday: a regionalism of Chiapas, sometimes used to call another person's attention.